THE LOST HERD

Archie Joscelyn

AVALON BOOKS

THOMAS BOUREGY AND COMPANY, INC.
22 EAST 60TH STREET • NEW YORK 10022

PRINTED IN THE UNITED STATES OF AMERICA
BY THE BOOK PRESS, BRATTLEBORO, VERMONT

The Lost Herd

1

"I ain't a prayin' man—not ordinarily"—the little man was as earnest as a robin tugging at a reluctant early worm—"nor yet a church-going sort, what with the nearest church more miles distant than I can count, even with my shoes off. But you happenin' along and droppin' in this way, Harry—" Jeb Cooley sucked a long breath. "Man, it's sure an answer to prayer, if ever anything was!"

Harry Blanchard smiled at his friend, his thoughts a mixture of affection and curiosity. It had been more design than chance that had brought him this way, but not for the world would he have admitted it. Cooley's mounting excitement and manifest relief that he had turned up rather surprised him. For all the nature of rumor and report, Jeb—prospector, trapper, rancher—was as self-sufficient a man as he had ever known.

"Reckon you're stretchin' things considerably, or else you've got me mixed up with somebody else," he returned with a faint smile. "But it's as nice to be welcome as it is to see you again. I was sort of between jobs, and the notion struck me that I could come see you, laze around a spell, soak up some sun."

He had no intention of admitting to traveling half a thousand miles, from Montana territory to Washington country, because word had reached him that his old friend had fallen on hard times and might need a leg up, physically or mentally.

"What'd I just say?" Cooley rejoined. "You comin' along this way right when I need you—it's sure providential. Though I reckon you won't mind delayin' loafin' and lappin' up the sun for a few days, not till we've taken us a little *pasear*—say, on the trail of the lost herd, just in case anybody should get curious as to where or why," he added with a grin.

"Lost herd?" Blanchard repeated. "You mean some of your stock have strayed?"

"These wan't mine, and they did it before ever I took over this ranch. Other things took mine off, such as the hard winter and harder-hearted creditors, but the lost herd's a good enough excuse for what ain't anybody's business."

"Just what's it all about, Jeb?" Beneath the banter of the old man's tone, Blanchard detected a deadly seriousness. "Some problem you need to curry?"

"If it was just one I'd ride it roughshod. This is like clubbin' one rattler, only to have a dozen more start waggin' their ugly tails at you. Guess I better tell you all about it—startin' with the good. So feast your eyes on that."

He tugged a beaded bag of soft buckskin from a pocket, loosened the drawstring, and extracted a picture—a tintype of a woman, remarkable not only for its clearness but for the beauty of the face that looked out. Wide, large eyes, serious but with the promise of a smile, an expectant eagerness lurking at the corners of her mouth.

"That's Mavis," Cooley explained. He was at once diffident but proud. "Ain't scarcely believable that I could have a daughter like that, eh?"

"She's lovely," Blanchard admitted. "I'd almost forgotten about your family back East."

"There's some things a man don't talk about." The words were starkly revealing. "It's almost as though my marriage never had been—except for her. Happened near a quarter of a century back. Both of us was young and impulsive. She was out here from the East, visitin' relatives, and I just happened to be handy when her horse ran away from her. Nothin' to brag about, but I guess I seemed sort of glamorous to her. Our marriage didn't last much longer'n it takes for dust to settle. She found she didn't like anything about the West, includin' me. So she went back to her folks.

"Now and then, as I could afford, I've sent her money. Like you know, I've made a couple of good strikes, prospectin'—only to lose them again. And the ranch here has paid pretty well, up to this last winter. So I've managed to support them in not too bad a style. Now—Mavis is a young lady, and her mother's gone. She writes that she wants to come see me, which I'd sure like."

Carefully he returned the photo to its container, then to his pocket.

"Trouble is, Harry, what with a hard winter and hard luck hittin' me high and low, I ain't rightly got nothing for her to come home to. Unless I get my paws on some hard cash, I'll be as broke as a snapped stick. Which ain't no way to receive a high-toned lady, 'specially your own daughter, who sounds like she thinks you're something special."

Blanchard now understood something that had always puzzled him—how such a supposedly well-to-do man could spend so much money and have so little to show for it. It was obvious that Jeb had supported his wife and daughter in elegant style. Supplying them with money from mortgaged land and cattle, when all else failed, confident that somehow he'd make another strike. . . .

The ranch was cumbered by a mortgage, its herds depleted almost to the vanishing point. Its actual worth was many times the debt, but times were hard, panic in the air nationally as well as locally; money was hard to come by.

"Which adds up to a good deal for a skinflint who holds the mortgage and has the chance to take over," Cooley added grimly. "But I've got a notion on how to fool him. I've been studyin' on another prospectin' trip for quite some while, and have the details worked out in my mind. Back in country I've seen but not what you'd call explored. All I need is a few weeks, this summer, back in there, time to look around and study one or two things out, and I'll make those earlier strikes look like small potatoes!"

Knowing Cooley, Blanchard was inclined to

accept what in most men would seem wild boasting. Since Jeb had visited that country, and was convinced that he was on the trail of something big, his reputation was a pretty good guarantee.

"There're problems in the way—or was, till you showed up," Cooley went on. The guileless eyes in a leathery face had a baby-blue look of innocence.

"I've been studyin' on this proposition for quite a spell, working out a few puzzlin' angles, and a while back, when I figured I had the answers, blamed if I didn't do a bit of celebratin'. Which was a plumb fool thing to do, but I told myself that just one drink wouldn't hurt. I hadn't properly wet my whistle for goin' on a year." He looked properly sheepish.

"Only some of your friends bought you a few more," Blanchard supplied.

"Well, friends is puttin' it pretty strong, though for a while I looked on them with a kindly eye and talked with a braggin' tongue. Reckon I boasted of what I had in mind. I couldn't tell too much, for there's plenty that I don't know yet, but I guess I sure enough overplayed my hand. They've a suspicion as to what I have in mind to try, and, since I've made some good strikes in the past, why, they figure that I can just maybe cut the mustard one more time.

"So now they're watchin' me like cats at a mouse hole. If I stir to get back to that country and go about my business, I know good and well they're all set to trail me. Course they'd set back and let me do the work, but the minute I make my strike, they aim to jump me and the claim."

Simple as it was in outline, that was an old game, but deadly.

"I've been schemin' how to outguess them, and with you showin' up, that provides the answer," Cooley went on. "You and I will go ridin', and sort of lose ourselves. And only you will come back. We'll get where I want to go, with such supplies as I'll need for the summer. They'll try to trail you, of course, but I know how that will work—same as catchin' smoke."

Blanchard was getting the picture. They could probably obtain a few hours' start, but others would discover their absence and follow, or at least do their best to pick up the trail. That part did not worry him any more than it did Cooley. It would require better than average trackers to sort out the sign they could provide.

If others did manage to follow, he would lead them astray, leaving Cooley to his summer for unmolested exploration.

"Sounds workable," he conceded. "But what if something goes wrong, with you way back from nowhere, all alone?"

"I've figured that angle, too," Cooley assured him. "I got myself a couple of these carrier pigeons. Been lookin' after the little buggers for quite some while. Have a pair of woven cages to take them along in. If anything goes wrong, I'll fasten a note to the legs of each, and send them back. You'll be here to get the mail, so to speak, and you'll know where to look for me. With you on the job, it don't add up to no undue risk.

"And of course, with you helping me this way, we'll be partners on whatever I find. No arguin', now, that's only fair. And no sweat, neither. If I find what I figure has sure enough got to be there, it'll make most strikes look like tobacco money."

2

Trouble erupted just when Blanchard felt that the risk was all but past. They had been followed, precisely as Cooley had known they would, but their planning, combined with Blanchard's skill at covering or confusing a trail, had seemed effective.

The trio who followed had been named by Cooley: Jim Kearns, Cloud, and Silverman, hangers-on, eager with the hope of an added wage. None were satisfied with an honest one.

Rifle shots spat without warning, perhaps from pure spite, but no less murderous on that account.

The first bullet gusted past Harry Blanchard's face, apparently aimed for the broad target of chest and shoulders. It was so close that Blanchard felt its deadly breath coursing past his cheek, even while he heard the rifle's coughing roar.

That came from surprisingly close, proof that at least one of the trio of pursuers had almost caught up, and whether by skill or chance no longer mattered. Afoot at the moment, Blanchard ducked instinctively, feet suddenly hurrying in the mud underfoot. It was greasy, so that he sprawled—thus saving his life, as the succeeding shots, even better aimed, growled past through the space he had so lately quitted.

His mind reacted as swiftly as his impulses. Those shots had been a mistake, for whatever reason. He doubted that Jim Kearns would approve or yield to such temptation, however tempting. Kearns was the boss because he was the planner, cold-blooded and with matching foresight. He was ready at any time to take a chance if the reward promised to be worthwhile, but never recklessly or blindly.

Cloud was stolid, slow, deadly when in action, but not one to act on impulse.

Back in here, as wildly high and rugged a country as Blanchard had ever seen, crowding among mountains in the north and west of Washington, it was remote enough to take a chance. That indicated Silverman.

The anger that had prompted the shots was easy to understand. They confirmed that Blanchard had done a good job of leading them astray, well away from Jeb Cooley. For a week they had trailed Jeb and himself; reading their sign, convinced of it, Blanchard had allowed them to follow, finally leading them widely, confusing them hopelessly.

Now, realizing how he had tricked them, supposing that any of his possible usefulness was past, Silverman, on catching sight of him, had vented his frustration.

Rain had commenced three days before, and the downpour had helped loosen the soil. But Silverman had been more skilled, or lucky, than Blanchard had expected.

Rolling into a cover of brush, Blanchard regained his feet. If Silverman figured that he had gone down from a hit and reacted accordingly . . .

Silverman was doing exactly that, running eagerly and openly. His weapon had been a rifle, but he was narrowing the distance to six-gun range. Blanchard shot high, by way of warning.

Reaction was as ludicrous as a fox, pouncing at prey and finding its paw suddenly in a trap. Silverman stopped, then was retreating, throwing aside his gun to make better speed. Blanchard lowered his own weapon in disgust.

An almost-full moon rode the sky, and out of its starlit spaces fluted the sounds of wild geese, coursing down from the north. Blanchard felt a stirring of blood, a quickening tempo to his thoughts. Aside from the usual chores, the summer at the ranch had been uneventful. But now it was the harvest moon, the season of change.

Kearns, Cloud, and Silverman, he knew, hung about the town, but no one paid much attention to them, and so long as they left him alone he had no desire to disturb them. If or when they crossed his trail again it could be a different story.

Geese! That the great birds should be fleeing the oncoming winter so unseasonably early triggered uneasy premonitions in Blanchard's mind. They flew by instinct, the breath of the arctic at their tails. They were a sure harbinger that summer was nearly at its end.

There had been no word from Jeb Cooley, but that seemed a good sign that he had been able to pursue his explorations unmolested. But with winter in the offing, he should be returning, or, failing that, should be sending word by the carrier pigeons. Though how they might prove in flight, after the long summer's inactivity, was a matter for guesswork, a reason for unease.

Until now, Blanchard had not worried. Jeb was good at looking out for himself; no man better. But accidents did happen, especially in far and lonely places. Now, with the wild geese heading south, his deadline was all but up.

In the hot sun of midday the blasting crash of a shotgun, coming without warning, spun him about. Normally he paid no attention, as the town was only a couple of miles away. An occasional popping of revolvers, as cowboys celebrated on a Saturday night, could be heard. But this was close by, on Jeb's land, the heavier cough that could belong only to a shotgun.

Blanchard was in time to see a fluttering object, suspended an instant in mid-air, then plummeting earthward amid a shower of feathers. With his mind already on his overdue partner, he sensed what was happening. One of the pigeons had been stopped just short of the house, by someone on the watch. Apparently the watchers had known about the birds and anticipated their return at least as eagerly as he.

Running toward the spot where the stricken bird had dropped from view, he saw Cloud coming from the opposite direction, still clutching the shotgun, determined to have the bird and whatever secret it might have carried.

Over my dead body, Blanchard thought, and realized that it could be literally so. Jerking at his holstered revolver, he shouted a warning, then, as Cloud plunged ahead lifting the muzzle of the shotgun, Blanchard fired first.

Cloud was too close, too heavy a figure to miss, and prudence warned that this time Blanchard should shoot to kill, as the shotgun would certainly do. Two things prevented. He had a compunction against killing if it could be avoided, and the situation here was different than well off in the wild when he had exchanged shots with Silverman. Out there, no questions would be asked. Here, with town right at hand, there would be inquiries, possibly charges of murder; in any case, it would bring on a lot of unwelcome publicity, causing a delay of days or weeks at the least, and if the pigeon was bringing a message from Jeb of trouble at his end, to come a-running . . .

Blanchard's confidence that he could put a bullet where he wanted it was again justified. He knew the numbing, shattering effect of a forty-five slug hammering against a steel barrel, and the double barrels of the scatter-gun, at the point where Cloud's big fingers clutched, made a perfect target. The howling scream of pain, as the weapon was wrenched loose, literally blasted from Cloud's numbed grasp, was added confirmation.

Normally slow-witted and lumbering of motion, Cloud had characteristics in common with a bear once he was in motion, lumbering ahead relentlessly, doggedly. Neither the loss of the shotgun nor the pain of the numbed hand slowed him. They reached the still-quivering mass of broken flesh and feathers at almost the same instant, and both men grabbed for the pigeon.

Blanchard was the quicker, but only by a fraction. As he closed his hand on the bird and snatched it back, Cloud's doubled to a fist. He smashed an uppercut toward Blanchard's chin, doubly savage as his stoop arose in time to the blow. Blanchard jerked his head aside, but rocklike knuckles, horny as the bark of a dead tree, slid along cheek and chin.

Even the edge of it was dazing, and somehow he had lost hold of his gun. Blanchard grabbed, dragging his foe to him, muffling his pumping fists as he fought in turn to clear his head, to retaliate. Still half-blind, he realized that Cloud was not alone, that the others of that unholy trio were swarming at and over him, a clubbed gun in the fingers of one of them. A desperate jerk of his head avoided the smash, only to meet one equally savage from the opposite side. The light seemed to go out in an explosive darkness punctuated by fireworks.

3

A throbbing ache at the back of his skull marked where that other blow had landed. Blanchard became aware of it as he worked back to consciousness, raising a hand to explore tenderly the swelling as he sat up, dizzy and sick. Memory was tardy in its own return.

Blinking uncertainly, he shrugged ruefully. The dead pigeon was gone, along with the trio who had assaulted him. Scattered feathers, a stain of blood, marked where the messenger had fallen. They had been after it, and they had gotten it.

Aside from the clubbing that had ended his part in the struggle, he had sustained no hurt. For that he gave unwilling credit to Kearns. Gentleman Jim would hardly have been actuated by sympathy in holding his more violent companions back from taking out their frustrations on a helpless foe; Kearns would have other, more practical motives for such restraint. The less time wasted in snatching up the dead bird and removing themselves from the scene and possible discovery, the better.

Blanchard's eyes focused on something, dusty and torn, not easily seen. He picked it up with quickening excitement, understanding. Kearns and his cohorts had been in too big a hurry.

During the struggle for possession of the dead bird, the small container, fastened to one of its legs, had been torn loose, to fall unnoticed on the ground.

They had helped themselves to his revolver, probably as a precautionary measure should he regain consciousness before they were out of sight. The shotgun was gone as well.

Resisting the impulse to have a quick look at whatever message the valiant little bird had carried, Blanchard got to his feet, moving shakily, heading for the house. No one else seemed to have been around to hear or see the disturbance. A few frost-touched leaves fluttered from a tree.

The news, whatever Jeb Cooley might have written, would almost certainly be bad. Otherwise he would have made it back by himself with the swift waning of summer, rather than resorting to what had admittedly been a last resort.

There was a stain of blood on the packet. Fumbling with fingers still clumsy, Blanchard wondered what it might hold.

Despite Cooley's former strikes, Blanchard was not at all sure that he believed in Jeb's dream of again being able to strike it rich. Even with Blanchard he had been ambiguous, though sure that he was on the trail of something big.

"I got a hunch about that wild country, off there to the northwest, right close up ag'in the border. I've even dreamed about it. It's like the poet puts it, of something lost beyond the mountains, waiting to be found. Well, I'm the man to find it. Who knows? I might even locate that lost herd of Slade Tatum's," he had added with a grin.

Blanchard had joined in the smile. Across a span of years, that disappearing herd had grown to the proportions of a legend, a shadowy mystery combining increasing rumor along with fact. It was nearly a decade since Slade Tatum had come to these parts, lingering just long enough to become a mystery in his own right.

Standing high even in a land of tall men, Tatum had possessed a look of elegance due only in part to the cut of his clothes and an arrogance of manner—a trait at odds with the furtiveness of his comings and goings, his not too well hidden fear of being robbed or even murdered. That reputation had been enhanced and partly explained by the report that he had a fortunc in gold, of which the actual ownership was in doubt.

How much, if any, truth might lie in such stories had been a subject for speculation, given a new twist when he had altered his look and manner as totally as a moth into butterfly, only in this case in reverse. The rich garments of a gentleman had disappeared, replaced by cotton shirt and bullhide chaps. With the change in clothes he had acquired a half-wild herd of cattle, three hundred or so, and had set out with a crew of two to drive them to market. It had amounted to a complete turnabout for a man reputed to be rich.

Even then the oddities had persisted. Instead of

striking south and east toward the distant railroad, Tatum had headed the herd into the northwest. Men and cows had quickly been swallowed by wilderness. The mystery had increased as the disappearance had become total.

"Yeah, a man just might do worse than follow in Tatum's steps," Jeb Cooley had continued, his grin widening. "I met old Slade a couple of times. And whatever else he may have been, he sure wan't a fool. He knew what he was about. Don't it strike you as all-fired funny the way a herd of that size, along with the men who drove 'em, could just up and disappear? I'll be keepin' an eye out for 'em," he had added with a wink, as Blanchard had prepared to head back to the ranch, leaving Cooley to his exploration and prospecting.

If such suppositions were fanciful, Cooley was not. He had dreamed a dream and followed a hunch. And now . . .

The message, soiled, almost illegible, was in Cooley's handwriting.

> I've got it, Harry, big as I'd hoped. But I sure need your help. I sent the other pigeon out near a week ago. Come a-runnin', boy.
>
> Jeb

The day's events were suddenly understandable. The first pigeon must have gotten through, perhaps falling somehow, at journey's end, into the hands of the unholy trio. And that too was an odd coincidence; there had been three with that lost herd, years before, that had so mysteriously disappeared.

Blanchard was not inclined to superstition, but like Cooley, he had a lot of respect for a hunch.

Now this bunch of men who operated at the fringe of the law knew that Jeb had made his strike, and they would expect him to respond to the call, hopefully this time to lead them to Jeb and his find.

Cloud, like Silverman at the start of the summer, had blundered. He should have left the second pigeon alone. Crafty Jim Kearns had worked to retrieve the blunder as much as possible. Looking anew at the missive, Blanchard revised his first guess and gave Kearns grudging credit. They had found and read it, all right, but it had been necessary for him to read it as well.

Now they would be twice as crafty, doubly dangerous. But with winter on the march, Jeb Cooley in trouble, he had to respond, and fast.

4

Since some hours of daylight remained, Blanchard moved unhurriedly, having planned already for such a contingency. His next chore seemed mundane—mixing a double pan of biscuits, building up the fire in the kitchen range, and sliding them into the oven. He left a note of instructions for his fellow cowhands, busy at the far end of the range. He had already given them general orders, should he take off suddenly.

If Cooley had made another big strike, he would be anxious for Blanchard to arrive. Getting the situation in hand, they would stake claims, then get back out and record them, making them legally theirs. The problem was what lay between.

Kearns, Cloud, and Silverman would be ready for whatever move he made, ready to follow, but doing their best to keep out of sight. Their preferred method of prospecting was to keep back while others made a discovery, then move in after the manner of jackals.

Blanchard went to the barn and bridled a pair of

horses, throwing a saddle on one. He slung a pack saddle on the other and piled it with supplies long-since readied—items such as blankets, a small tent, cooking utensils, beans, bacon and flour, tinned goods—then strapped the goods into place.

He ate supper and packed the fresh store of biscuits. By this time dusk was at hand as he returned to the barn. A third pony neighed eagerly as he started with the others, and on impulse he threw another saddle across its back.

"So you'd like to go along too? Well, why not? I can travel faster with change-offs. And who knows? Jeb may have lost his horse."

He led the three out through a back door, tying them among a clump of aspen. Save for a last-minute chore, which must be delayed until night darkened into a heavier cloak against possible spying eyes, everything was in readiness for takeoff.

Leaving the aspens, he threaded a loose strand of evergreens, glancing in passing at a mechanical contraption of log and plank that had puzzled Jeb upon first finding it; unused for a decade, it still left him wondering. It was a solidly built chute into which a steer or cow, even a full-grown and strongly resisting animal, could be driven or dragged, to be solidly prisoned as the movable side was clamped against it by the pull of a lever. Held so, virtually unable to move, an animal could be vaccinated, branded, or even dehorned with a minimum of risk or trouble.

Jeb had been away from his new ranch when someone had built it. On his return, he found the chute and evidence that it had been much used. Report had it that Slade Tatum, in his new role as cattleman, had taken the liberty of using Cooley's corrals in his absence, then had clearly run his animals through the chute.

They had been gone when Jeb returned, and the possible reason for such odd conduct was one more of the unanswered mysteries surrounding the lost herd.

Shrugging without much interest for the old riddle, Blanchard headed back, glancing where sunset flamed red across the west. It would soon be dark. Excitement quickened his blood. Since that foray with Cooley, he had put in a long summer of hard work, doubly tiring as the watching had increased, and it would be pleasant to get away for a few days.

He checked as a flash of color caught his eye, staring with surprise and a doubtful pleasure. Visitors were few at any time, and for a woman to come was doubly rare. But this surprising caller was a woman—or, at second thought, scarcely more than a girl. She was pleasantly eye-filling, somehow familiar.

Right now he would have preferred not to be bothered by anyone, even so breath-taking a visitor. She turned at his step, took a quick step, then waited.

That she was as new to this country as to his ranch, Blanchard decided in his first quick appraisal. She seemed a bit flashily dressed, as newcomers are apt to be. Though her outfit appeared serviceable, beginning with boots of soft leather into which mannish jeans were tucked, topped by a soft shirt, encased by a red and black mackinaw. A wide white felt hat covered a wealth of hair as golden as the treasure sought by Jeb Cooley.

She watched his approach frankly, a shade of impatience gathering between her eyes. Those matched the darkening blueness of the sky, though that might be a trick of the light. Blanchard's already quickened pulse drummed a little faster.

Appraising in turn, she saw a tall man, walking with the easy swing of a cowboy who was also accustomed to using his own legs. His uncovered head disclosed brown hair whose natural curl would be the envy of most women, steady gray eyes looking out from under. For the rest, he was lean and brown, with an unconscious air of competence.

Latent impatience came to the fore as his pace continued unhurried.

"Are you the man known as Handsome Harry?"

Blanchard nodded warily. How would she know that, when few did? The title had been affectionately bestowed upon him by Jeb Cooley.

"I've been called that," he acknowledged.

"Then you are Harry Blanchard?"

He nodded, increasingly puzzled. She saw that his dark hair showed a slight thinning above the forehead, and judged his age at a half more than her own. Despite that hint of baldness, he seemed almost boyish.

"That's right," he agreed. "I'm Blanchard."

Her next words staggered him.

"Then," she said, and it was a command rather

than request, "you will please take me to my father at once, Harry Blanchard. Or I'll have the law on you!"

Almost as an afterthought, coloring slightly as though suddenly aware of her rudeness, she added, "I'm Mavis Cooley. Jeb Cooley is my father."

5

"And are you so, now?" That, or a similar retort, would have been Cooley's response to so surprising a declaration, and it came to Blanchard that this girl was in some respects as unpredictable as her father. He could discern the resemblance, though that Jeb's daughter might take a notion to come West and visit her father without notification had not occurred to him—nor, he was sure, to Jeb. Otherwise, Cooley would certainly have mentioned the possibility and prepared accordingly, before setting out for a long and lonely summer.

"Mavis," he repeated, then was at a loss. Readiness of retort might rise in his mind, but it did not get easily past his tongue.

Now he could see the same determined chin, offset by a wide, good-natured mouth. Her eyes were challenging, but with a hint of uncertainty. That was somehow in keeping with the saucy uptilt to the nose. But where Cooley was rugged, she possessed a softness that even such an air of assertiveness could not offset.

Blanchard had heard tales of Mavis since the early days of their acquaintanceship, when Cooley's wide experience had proved invaluable. Jeb Cooley had talked wistfully of going East to visit her, or of bringing her West—vague dreams that somehow never materialized.

By long-distance Cooley had almost blindly adored her, but considering himself incapable of properly raising a girl child, he had contented himself with sending money for her upkeep as fortune allowed. Someday, when he made his new strike, it had been his dream to bring her to his country, to show her its rugged beauty—though of course only during the mild season of summer. He was determined that the hardships that to him were routine should never touch her.

So unannounced an arrival at this particular time was doubly startling. With her father gone through the summer there could have been no correspondence. Perhaps it was the lack of any word for so long that had worried her, though Blanchard could recall no letter from her since early the previous spring. Whatever the reason, she had taken a notion to come West and see for herself.

As a child she had probably been content to dream, but now she was a woman, capable of translating thought into action, strongly determined. As events were turning out, her coming might be frosting to Cooley's cake. Having made his find, he would be more than delighted to share with her.

Blanchard drew a slow breath, striving to set his thoughts in order. "So you're Mavis," he repeated, and held out his hand. "I'm flabbergasted, to put it mildly. But I'm glad to see you, and to welcome you to this part of the country—"

Pointedly she ignored his hand. Her voice lost none of its chill, her eyes none of their suspicion.

"I would like to believe that was so, but I take leave to doubt it. What have you done to my father?"

Almost in her first breath she had threatened him with the law. There was more in this than a lack of understanding. Blanchard's hand dropped.

"Done with him?" he repeated. "Now, why should I have done anything with him?"

"You can't put me off that way, Mr. Blanchard, as though I were a small child," she warned. "I have reason to believe that you *have* done something, and that you are trying to cheat him, or perhaps worse. It's known to your neighbors and everyone in the town that the two of you disappeared months ago under mysterious, not to say questionable, circumstances. Later you turned up again, without explanation, but no one has seen or heard of my father since!"

Blanchard stared, beginning to understand, then burst out laughing. It would have been like Cooley to have told her nothing of his plans when he had last written her, though he might have hinted at his hopes. He had the true prospector's sense of secretiveness, the desert rat's conviction that the fewer who knew what was up, the better. Aside from Blanchard, who had assisted and was his partner in the enterprise, no one else had been told a word.

No longer a child, Mavis clearly had worried. When the weeks had lengthened into months, she had acted on impulse, taking a train west, transferring to a stage, finally arriving at the town a few miles away, and making inquiries. The answers she had received, ignorant or possibly malicious, had strengthened her suspicions and compounded her fears.

"I guess I can't blame you for being worried," Blanchard agreed. "You're right, we did more or less slip away, as mysteriously as we could manage. That was your dad's idea, and I agreed. We've been partners, more or less, especially in prospecting, and I helped him in this. He had a hunch—call it a notion he'd worked out, from quite a few things—that he knew where to make one more big strike. He needed the summer to work in, and of course he had to be able to work alone, without anyone who would be anxious to jump his claim the minute he found it spying. So we contrived to disappear one night, and I came back alone."

He hesitated at revealing more, but she had a right to know, and he could not see how it could do any harm.

"I've been more or less hoping and expecting him back for the last few weeks. But I just got word this afternoon that he's had a mix of luck, some good and some not so nice. He's made his strike, but he says he needs help. So I've been getting ready to head back where I left him and lend a hand. I've horses saddled and packed, and if you hadn't found me just as you did, I'd have been gone, with no one the wiser."

Mavis listened, watching him closely, a play of emotions across her face. Clearly, this was not at all the sort of answer she had expected.

"Then he's all right? Nothing has happened to him?"

"I told you that he needs help. So something has happened, though I don't know what. He asked me to come a-running—which I intend to do."

Her initial truculence was gone. "But where is he?" The suspicion was back in her eyes.

"He'd been preparing for this expedition for quite a while, and one of his safeguards was to train homing pigeons. We took a pair of them along last spring. One pigeon came back a couple of hours ago with his message, just as I've told you. He said he'd got it—meaning, I take it, that he'd made his strike, the way he hoped, but that he needed help, and for me to come running."

Night was closing as they talked. Mavis frowned, white teeth worrying a vivid underlip. Her retort surprised him.

"Then, if you're going to find and help him, I'm going with you. He's my father."

"Go . . . with me, back beyond nowhere?" Blanchard was aghast. "You don't know what you're talking about."

"Meaning that you don't want anybody along, not even me, even if I am his daughter?"

"Oh, good Lord," Blanchard protested. "You just don't understand. I'm traveling alone, and fast. It won't be any pleasure jaunt. And if I took you, we'd be alone."

Her mouth quirked in a sudden half smile, then was stern again.

"I can hold up my end, Harry Blanchard, and I'm willing to risk the hardships. As for being with you, that doesn't worry me. Father has sung your praises in his letters for almost as long as I can remember. I'm sure I can trust you to be a gentleman."

His blunt answer shocked her almost as much as she had startled him. "Thanks for that. But you don't know what you're asking. I can't afford to be held up or slowed down. And to be honest, I like to know what I'm doing, and whom *I* can trust."

Anger blazed at him in eyes and voice. "Are you implying, Harry Blanchard, that you can't trust me?"

"Wouldn't the feeling be mutual?" he countered, then his smile became a grin, suddenly warm. "You're holding something back—something that you haven't told me, and I don't like misunderstanding. And it wouldn't just happen. Somebody's been talking to you, or maybe writing letters, filling your head with a lot of wrong notions. For your father's sake, as well as yours—and my own—I can't afford to take chances, to go it blind. I might chance the delays and risks attendant to having you along, but I have to know what's going on—what's really in back of this big, sudden decision on your part. He'd never forgive me if I didn't."

"What—how do you mean?" Though still challenging, her voice held a quality of uncertainty.

Blanchard glanced about, making sure even in the gathering dusk that there should be no eavesdroppers.

"I took Jeb where he wanted to go, without letting

anyone else know. That was the way he wanted it. He still wouldn't want anyone else—except maybe you—to find out. There are others who would give a right arm for the chance to jump his claim, to register it before he could."

His earnestness seemed to convince her.

"Maybe—perhaps I've been mistaken..."

"Could be," he agreed cheerfully. "We all make mistakes. But I'd sure like to know who's been filling your head with a lot of crazy notions."

For a moment, she seemed on the point of telling him. Then the uncertainty returned to her eyes.

"I—I was told some things, but they were confidential, and I agreed to keep them so. If my conclusions were wrong—and it begins to look as though they may have been—then when I'm sure, I'll be more than happy to change them, even to apologize. But I can't break my word."

She was like her father, loyal to a trust. Blanchard's eyes clouded. He was beginning to get the picture. Someone—and he could easily guess who—had written to her, angling for any possible information she might possess or be tricked into revealing. The culprit had dropped hints that something was up, and had met and talked to her after her arrival in town. All of which added up to a situation not at all to Blanchard's liking.

Whatever he might do now would be risky, but he dared not delay. When old Jeb asked for help, and fast, it must be given. He was far from happy at the notion of being encumbered with a traveling companion, especially with the responsibility for the girl's safety, but he had to take her along. If he refused, she would believe the worst, and would almost surely do something to attract attention. That would ruin the precautions he had already taken, which now were more necessary than ever. Others had already meddled, hoping among other things to circumvent Cooley and himself by bringing her into it.

His only chance was to take off at once, and for that, luckily, his preparations had been completed, and they were sufficient for both. She could ride the extra horse, occupy the tent at night. Supplies were ample. And no one would be expecting such a move or ready to counter it.

Hesitation or delay would play into their hands, giving them time to arrange a counterplay. He made up his mind.

"Fair enough. I respect such a commitment, but I want one in return. That, if I take you along, you'll not make any sign that others might be able to follow, or try to give them a lead as to where we're heading for. That would betray your father most of all. And we'll travel fast and hard. It won't be any holiday excursion."

This time, she extended her hand, clasping his own in a warm, firm grip.

"That's fair, too. I'll hold up my end, I promise. When do we start?"

His answer surprised and startled her.

"Now. The horses are ready. No time to waste, even to get any articles you might want."

"Can I take this much?" She picked a compact

bundle from the edge of the path. "I had it ready—just in case."

"You know," Blanchard returned, "I reckon you *are* Jeb's girl, in more ways than one." He thought briefly of the collection of flasks that, almost as an afterthought, he had tucked away deep inside the duffle. The liquor had been a gift, untouched till now. It had occurred to him that a dram of whiskey might come in useful if Jeb was hurt or sick.

Should Mavis discover such cargo, she might get a wrong notion. But that was a slight chance among the many.

6

Blanchard moved fast, in deep blackness before the moon would rise, hoping to get the jump on his enemies. Almost certainly they would count on Mavis slowing him down for hours or even a day or more. She followed close behind, but the arrangement precluded conversation, which at the moment was necessary.

He accepted her disclaimer that she was not actively leagued with Kearns, but that Gentleman Jim had learned of her and gotten in touch with her, inducing her to come West at this particular time, intent on using her as a cat's-paw in the furtherance of his schemes, was not to be doubted. The distrust, even hostility that she had shown, had been carefully planted and nourished.

A few minutes' riding satisfied him that she was at home in the saddle, and that was reassuring. With Cooley in trouble, he had to push hard. Other reasons were equally imperative. Not even her weariness or discomfort could hold them back.

His initial irritation at her demand to be taken along was mitigated as he understood her concern, but not entirely. A refusal on his part would have confirmed her suspicions, leading to more delays and difficulties.

This first night, even the first few miles, could prove vital. He had planned carefully for such a contingency, and he hoped to trick their trackers, by obtaining a lead that could not be overcome, then vanishing so completely that they could not be followed. That it would take some doing was certain, for Kearns and his men were skilled and determined. If he fooled them tonight they would discover his absence by morning, and try to follow. That would not be easy, even for skilled trackers, but he did not underestimate Kearns.

Even if they found sign, they would have no way of knowing who had made it; but by ranging widely enough to pick up the trail of three horses, once beyond settled country, they could make a pretty accurate guess. Before then, he intended to cover and confuse the trail.

Moonrise was belated, and the thin disc was almost lost among clustering stars. Night sounds were familiar and friendly to his ears—but this was his country, and Cooley's. He looked back to smile reassuringly at Mavis at the devastating shriek of a screech owl and felt a rush of approval as she waved. It increased, surprise giving way to incredulity as the miles fell behind and she voiced no protests, asked no questions. Whatever her upbringing, she was her father's daughter.

Finally they splashed into a stream and the horses lowered their heads to drink. Hers pushed alongside, and as he had a good look, tiredness was unmistakable both in her face and sagging shoulders. Suddenly contrite, Blanchard realized how far they had come, how grueling the ordeal. No one could have done better at keeping pace, and however well she rode, she could hardly be trail-toughened.

"Can I take time to get a drink too?" she asked, stirring wearily.

"Of course," he said, "I didn't realize . . ."

The moon was waning, which meant that it was past midnight. She was clearly played out, but too proud to protest. Abruptly he changed his plans. Jeb's daughter deserved consideration, as well as Jeb himself.

"We'll get a few hours' sleep," he decided. "I'll set up the tent for you."

It was small, and he had it ready in a matter of minutes, managing in the process to clip an armful of spruce branches from the base of trees that stood conveniently close. Arranging them, with an extra blanket to serve in lieu of mattress, he knew that it wouldn't make too much difference; tired as she was, she would sleep easily.

Beyond a heart-felt sigh at his pronouncement she had said nothing more, only sliding stiffly from the saddle, then stooping to drink from her hands. She gave him a wan smile as he announced that her quarters were ready.

"Thank you," she said. "Good night." She was certainly game, and uncomplaining. Because he had more or less expected protests or questions, he had overreacted.

With the horses picketed, he wrapped himself in a blanket and was quickly asleep. His original intention to snatch only a couple of hours' rest he discarded. She needed a good sleep, and when it came to that, so did he. The trail was a long one.

Sun on his face awakened him. It filtered through a rift in evergreen branches overhead, and he sat up half guiltily. The morning was crisp and cool. No stir came from the tent, but the horses, picketed in a small meadow nearby, were restless, having grazed off the grass within the radius of their ropes.

Cooley's ranch had been left well behind, and already they were into unsettled, largely unclaimed country. That was a condition he liked, though he realized that it could not much longer continue. All the land had been wild when Jeb had pushed past boundaries to claim his own land, choosing a ranch fitted to his needs. In the ensuing decade a town had grown almost at his doorstep, and neighbors were encroaching. From now on, the process of settlement was bound to accelerate.

But for now it remained unspoiled, and occasional trees afforded cover. There was no good reason, he decided, against a fire, small and almost smokeless, over which to boil coffee and fry bacon. He could picture his companion's awakening as tantalizing aromas drifted across to the tent. If her appetite was half as sharp as his . . .

Apparently it was. He heard movement as the coffee boiled, and Mavis stepped outside as he stirred the crisping bacon. She looked rested, eager, and somehow she had contrived to look neat and fresh.

"Good morning," she said. "I smelled the bacon—and I'm starved!"

"Then dig in," he invited, as he filled a tin plate and poured black coffee into a matching cup. "We've no sugar or cream—"

"After missing supper, who needs them?" Mischief glinted in her eyes. "Your response to my request rather caught me off-guard, but after I'd been so demanding, I couldn't suggest any delay."

Blanchard stared, a biscuit suspended between plate and mouth. Again he felt a rush of consternation.

"Good Lord! And I didn't even think about it. You must be wondering what your dad ever found to like about me for a partner—"

"I'm beginning to understand why he would ask you to come a-running!"

Soberly he poured second cups of coffee. "I hope you slept well."

"Like a log. I'd never dreamed—oh, this country is glorious!" She stretched shapely arms in a wide gesture. Later, riding alongside him, she amplified.

"It's so big. Everything about this land. I'm just beginning to understand why my father loves it so. Mother used to say that he was a true pioneer, who would have been right at home as a mountain man or in a covered wagon. And I guess he had some experience of both. She finally came to the conclusion that he couldn't stand being cooped up in a city, or even a town—not for long."

"Towns give him cabin fever," Blanchard agreed. "He didn't like even the ranch for very long at a time. He has to have room to move around in—and his idea of room is a hundred miles beyond the nearest neighbor."

"He sometimes wrote something of how he felt," Mavis agreed. "He was almost poetic, making me feel it, too. So, when my mother passed on just last spring and there was nothing more to keep me in the East, I decided to head this way and surprise Dad. I thought he'd like it, and I wanted to see him, to get to know him, as well as the country. Now I can begin to understand what it means to him."

She was giving him the main explanation of her unannounced arrival. She went on frankly.

"I had to ask questions when I reached town, to find my way—and some of the answers I received were disturbing. Some men, like Mr. Sam Anderson, liked you. That was easy to see. Others—well, after what you've told me, I can see *why* they might not like you too well."

Blanchard was impressed by her honesty. Reaching the town, after a tiring journey, confused and seeking advice, chance or mischance—perhaps prior information—had led to some who had filled her head with innuendoes and misconceptions, and deliberately. More than likely, though she hesitated to reveal that much, one or several letters had given her the notion of coming West, to look after her father, portrayed as a too-trusting man in danger of being victimized by his partner.

She had sought him out, with a chip on her

shoulder. Still not completely certain, she remained reticent on some points, but she was obviously anxious to be fair. It had not escaped him that she now referred to Cooley as Dad, rather than the more formal Father, which perhaps indicated, though indirectly, a greater acceptance of himself.

Though alert, he rode with increasing confidence. So far as he could tell, they had eluded any pursuers. Not that he intended to relax his vigilance. Others would have no doubt of where they headed, though the location remained to be discovered.

"It's wild and rugged country, where I left your dad," Blanchard explained. "Not the sort where I'd look to find gold. But he knows a lot more about prospecting than I do, and besides that, he plays hunches. And quite often, they turn out to be right."

"But what sort—I mean, what really is a hunch?" she asked, bewildered.

"A hunch is something, a feeling or instinct, that a man keeps to himself—or at least Jeb does. All that I know about this one is that he has a notion to find something in that part of the country, and my notion is that it seems to have some connection with the lost herd. Though that may be just a bit of window-trimming, to keep anyone from stumbling on to what he really is about."

"The lost herd? What on earth is that?"

"It's rather on a par with the rest, and real enough, though a lot of it doesn't quite make sense. Soon after Jeb settled on his ranch, a man known as Slade Tatum came along. Nobody knew much about him, and he was as tight-jawed as a steel trap. Still, the report got around that he was carrying a fortune—maybe in gold coins, or even nuggets. Anyhow, a fortune. Also that he was scared half to death by somebody who intended to rob him, and more than likely kill him in the process."

Mavis shivered.

"What a—a gruesome tale!"

"Such happenings were common enough. The strange part is that, instead of traveling for other parts as fast as he could, Tatum bought some cattle that another man was driving, two or three hundred head. He built a chute or squeeze-pen on your dad's land, for branding or dewlapping stock, and they say that he burnt his brand of a Double Diamond on each cow and steer. The evidence seems to back that up.

"With the branding done, and a couple of helpers, they took off, driving the herd. And that's where the real mystery begins. The herd and the men disappeared, vanishing as though the earth had swallowed them. Sign indicated that they had headed north by west—the same as we're doing. Now there's the tradition of the lost herd, since they were never seen again; nor was Tatum or the others of his crew."

Mavis drew a long breath.

"And Dad has some sort of a notion—a hunch, based on that? But it's incredible. . . ."

"Sure is," Blanchard agreed cheerfully. "Whether there's any real connection, beyond the fact that there was such a herd and that it headed this way and was lost, *quien sabe?* As I say, he was more than likely talking through his hat, sort of throwing dust in the eyes of anybody who might try to look too closely at what he was really doing. Still, the herd went that a-way—and, ten years later, he had the hunch to explore off that way."

"And you can find him again—off in such wild and trackless country?"

"There's not likely to be much trouble about that. It's what sort of trouble he may have gotten into that worries me. But he figured to be all right, once I arrived, so we'll make it so."

She found it reassuring that he knew what he was doing, a man at home in such an immense country. Apparently there were no streams, at least not running in the proper direction, for boats or canoes. On foot, she guessed that one would be lost and all but helpless.

It came to her that she should be apprehensive, with only this man's skill to avert disaster, not alone for her father but for herself. But, curiously, she was not. Her father had made clear in his letters that he had complete confidence in Harry Blanchard, and she was beginning to understand why.

7

This was wild country, with evidences of civilization left behind. Mavis could understand its appeal to a man like her father, a primeval attraction. But it seemed to her to harbor a threat, some sort of evil. It was only a feeling, but she could better understand a hunch and how it could grow almost to a conviction.

Blanchard was alert for any indication of pursuit, though he did not fool himself that the lack of sign insured safety. Kearns and his men would almost certainly have tried to follow, and even if they failed to pick up the trail, they might follow a hunch of their own and hope to stumble upon Cooley or his camp by a law of averages. And if such a gamble paid off, he and Mavis and probably Cooley would be a long way from friends or help.

His own premonition was that it would be so, and he blamed himself for yielding to Mavis's entreaties, for risking her safety under such circumstances. Of course, she had demanded more than asked, and it had seemed the easiest way to solve the dilemma, to avoid costly delays. But he might have temporized, then gotten away by himself, without her. . . .

With each day, each added span of miles, as he came to know her better, his apprehensions increased. She was a pleasant companion, and she neither slowed him nor caused trouble, which in itself was rather wonderful. He liked having her along, even as he wished more and more that she was safe back in town. But it was too late to do anything about it.

Nature was at its best. Frost had painted brush and trees to a rainbow symphony, the streams ran softly, a winey tonic to the air. Under less hurried conditions Blanchard would have enjoyed it to the full. But his hunch was working overtime. He had seen nothing to indicate that Gentleman Jim and his cohorts were on their trail, but an unyielding sense, an instinct from dark days and blacker nights of time's beginning insisted that they were.

Landmarks, altered by the changing season, meaningless to eyes less attuned than his, warned that they were approaching the territory where he had left Jeb Cooley. It was time for trickery, and the place he had had in mind from the beginning was right ahead.

They emerged from a cover of great trees to a tangle of brush, then out from that to a hard rocky beach that left no hoofmarks as the horses took to water, following the equally rocky bed of a stream. It wound and twisted for more than two miles, before deep water ahead made it necessary to get back on dry land, but there again the ground left scant sign of passage. Another mile, and he drew a long breath of relief.

Prior to reaching the creek, he had taken what seemed like a wrong turn, a false swing. He left just enough sign that any who might follow would almost certainly be led in the obvious but wrong direction, with the two groups diverging ever more widely. If Cloud proved a skilled enough tracker to sort out the tangle, days would be lost in the doing—more than enough, with any luck, for their purposes.

One of the pack horses shied, eyes rolling in upflung head. It snorted fearfully, and an instant later the other animals were all but out of control, frightened by the same contagion. Mavis's question was low but strained.

"What is it?"

"They've caught a scent—some animal—"

He was as much reassured as surprised at a rumbling bellow from somewhere close at hand; he had heard similar bawls too many times to mistake a cow or bull, and the proximity of a half-wild creature might spook the horses. The surprise was that such a creature should be here, though there was a possible, even a reasonable explanation. It might be a survivor, a remnant from Slade Tatum's lost herd.

His half-formed hope that the fright of the cayuses sprang from nothing worse was as quickly smashed by an answer to the bellow—this a full-throated, deep-chested growl of uncertainty, verging on anger, another noise that, once heard, was not to be mistaken. Bear.

And, more than likely, a grizzly.

It would be the bear's scent that had terrorized the horses and was still rendering them hard to control. As to it being a grizzly rather than one of the lesser species, the answer was in that challenging roar. A black or cinnamon would emit a similar scent, but it would be likely to shy away rather than hunt for trouble. A grizzly might run, but it was just as likely to turn stubborn, even challenging.

The afternoon sun, filtered through all but leafless branches overhead, was warm for Indian summer; warm enough at least that sweat started on Blanchard's face as he pulled the Winchester from its sheath.

Those initial noises, question and challenge, meant precisely what he had feared. The deeper bellowing of the bull, almost overridden by the coughing roar of the grizzly, dissolved any doubt. An instant later both antagonists charged into view in an open glade hardly a hundred feet away. Coming from opposite directions, each looking for the other, both spoiling for a fight.

Given the nature of the critters, that was understandable. Nature was enjoying a lull, a restful period before the storms of winter, but for most creatures of the wild it was a time of apprehension, instinct warning them of cold and hunger close ahead. Nerves pulled taut, instincts raggedly ruthless. Bear or bull, each claiming mastery, was ready to fight at any provocation or merely for the sheer joy of battle.

With this pair it was easily understandable. The

bull stood lean but massive, his heavy winter coat a sorrel red, the horns that tipped a horny skull wide-sweeping, rapier-pointed. He had paused at the edge of the open to paw, head lowered, the gusty exhalation of nostrils lifting a spurt of dust. Blanchard estimated that he would weigh a good half-ton.

On his side, long a part of hair and pattern but unmistakably etched, was an ancient brand—a pair of wide-spreading diamonds.

Here was a survivor, a remnant across the years, of Tatum's vanished herd.

Any cow or bull that could fend for itself against all comers must inevitably become as much a creature of the wild as the grizzly; the longhorn of course had a heritage of the Texas bush, of generations of ancestors pitted against all perils of a wilderness.

The grizzly was an equally magnificent specimen of his kind. He too had paused an instant, coming erect, great paws outreaching, the massive claws like the tips to a Bowie knife. His weight would match the bull's.

Blanchard and Mavis were having their hands full, trying to control the horses. The girl's glance was apprehensive, yet excited. Blanchard shared it, with added reason. A wild bull could be unpredictable, a grizzly doubly so. Should anything divert its attention from the bull to themselves and their horses, perhaps the hated scent of human drifting on the air, it might turn suddenly, unpredictably, and charge them instead.

In such an eventuality, he would have no choice

except to empty the Winchester into the monster at point-blank range, hoping that it might stop short of a carnage that, even in its death-throes, could easily result in a mauling of horses and humans, a serious wounding or possible destruction of all. A wounded grizzly, maddened, did not succumb easily.

It was not a situation to his liking. With so much at stake, especially the safety of Mavis Cooley, he was pulling for the bull, hopeful that it could make good its challenge.

The preliminaries to battle could be drawn out, but this time they were brief. Each recognized a mortal enemy, a threat to be destroyed. Roaring and bawling, they charged almost as on signal, meeting with a crash at the middle of the ring.

It was a battle of giants, each animal the victor of other struggles for survival, both sure of themselves. A single stroke of the grizzly's paw, properly delivered, could break the back of a horse or cow, smashing it to the ground. A sweeping stroke of claws could disembowl with equal speed.

But the butting crash of the bull's head could knock even so huge an enemy into a spin, crushing, smashing. A gouge of a horn could rend to heart and vitals like the thrust of a sword in the hand of a skilled fencer.

Bellowing, growling, locked together, it was a clash of giants, too frenzied to last long. Blanchard made out the smash of a mighty paw, cleaving down like an axe. But even as the blow was being delivered, the horns of the bull were embedded, buried almost out of sight in the guts of the grizzly. They collapsed together, the bear on top, but both kicking in the final throes.

Silence returned, so suddenly that the air seemed to hum with the excitement of insects. The horses, sensing the passing of threat, calmed somewhat, though still snorting their dislike.

Blanchard slipped the rifle back in its container. Not at all to his surprise, his hands were shaky, now that it was all over. Mavis was white-faced, the excitement drained away. But she showed no sign of collapsing as he urged the more than willing horses ahead.

8

Blanchard was greatly relieved. He had held that water trail in reserve, an ace that might make all the difference, not alone to them but to Jeb Cooley and whatever were the fruits of his summer's work. It would have been a shame, perhaps a disaster, to have it spoiled by the necessity of using his rifle. Such sounds carried far.

Mavis's question showed that her mind was busy along the same lines as his own. She was suddenly curious about that lost herd, with what must be a survivor turning up so unexpectedly.

"What could such cattle—a lost herd—have to do with Dad's hunch for prospecting off here?" she asked, puzzled. "What possible connection could they have with him making a strike?"

"I've no idea," Blanchard admitted. "But Jeb has a gift for sniffing out odd factors, like a hound on a cold scent, then adding them up to make something. He should be in this vicinity, and apparently his hunch in regard to the herd worked out. But what part they could play, I just don't know."

"In his last letter to me, he was very tantalizing and mysterious. He said he had nothing more to go by than a bird did when it followed its instincts, emigrating halfway around the earth. But he added that if he was right, I might yet wear the diamonds his carelessness with earlier finds had cheated me out of. That has always been a half joke, half promise with him—that someday I'd wear diamonds."

"That sounds like him," Blanchard admitted. "Years ago, making or losing a fortune was all one to him. It wasn't the money that he was interested in, only the fun of making the strike. But with you growing up, I guess he got to worrying that he was somehow cheating you, that he should leave you a worthwhile inheritance, since otherwise there would only be memories, and not many of them."

"I don't care about the money." Mavis sighed. "All I want is to find him."

That might be more of a problem than Blanchard had expected. Cooley could have changed his camp during the summer; if he was lying somewhere, sick or hurt, Harry had little to go on. Normally, expecting Blanchard to respond, Jeb might send a smoke signal rising as a beacon, but circumstances might render that inadvisable, even impossible.

Sharply observant for any sign, he came upon some, ancient and weathered, but familiar. Almost overgrown by brush was another chute, a hand-operated squeeze press like the one on Jeb's own ranch. Both were long unused, this one almost lost amid a tangle of grass and weeds.

But that it was here showed that it had been built

with some purpose in mind, a strong indicator that the vanished herd must indeed have come this way. What use it could have been put to was the puzzling aspect. Tatum and his men had already branded the cattle before setting out. They would hardly have been rebranded.

None of that made sense, but apparently Jeb had worked out the answer, along with its significance. An answer that had perhaps gotten him into trouble.

Small meadows, intersected by coulees and clumps of timber, combined for a confusing pattern. Hills rose high, in imitation of mountains. A creek frothed and hurried, unlike the placid streams they had earlier crossed.

Mavis's ready smile of delight or pleasure had become less frequent, her silences prolonged. She turned now with almost a shiver of apprehension.

"It's so—so strange," she confessed. "It's almost frightening. I suppose I'm being silly, but somehow, I feel as though something was going to happen. . . . As though danger—oh, I don't know. But it is . . . strange."

Her horse pressed close to his, as though with the same sense of wrongness, and Blanchard was conscious of the same oppression. Before he could reply, they rounded a bluff, and before them, as he had been hoping and watching for, were the dead ashes of a campfire; of many fires, as a closer look disclosed, which was as it should be.

There were other evidences that Cooley had been there. A rocklike shelf was set in the bluff, and on that was an empty cage, handwoven of willows. Its door stood open, but a feather had caught in a crack.

"At least we've found his camp," Blanchard said. "So he can't be far off. That cage held the pigeons when we came in last spring."

"But it looks so—so deserted," Mavis protested.

"We knew that something was wrong," Blanchard reminded. He forced himself to shout, fighting an unusual hesitation. There was no response.

"No telling where he might be," he pointed out, trying to sound reassuring. "Sounds get swallowed up by the hills."

He refrained from mentioning other sign, all too clear to eyes as practiced as his own. Not just one person, but several, had been there, not too many days before. That supplied an answer of sorts as to why Cooley had sent out the pigeons, probably at the first opportunity, his urgent plea for help. Apparently he had made his strike, and these others, who had quite possibly been keeping out of sight but spying on him for days or weeks, had either known or at least guessed. . . .

Probably they had jumped him without warning, though he was too old a campaigner to be caught completely off-guard. The tone of his note indicated something of a stalemate. But what might have happened in the intervening days, especially if the others had realized that he had managed to send out a plea for help . . .

Prospecting the deserted camp for sign, much as Cooley might have examined a promising lead, Blanchard kicked a charred bone from among the ashes, then examined it with mounting interest.

Though quite dry, it was reasonably fresh. Seeing his interest, Mavis eyed it apprehensively.

"It—it isn't—does that have some meaning to you?"

"It's an animal bone," he assured her. "The interesting part is that it's a beef bone. Somebody killed a steer or cow—and it's more proof of cattle being back in here."

"Somebody?" She caught him up, and Blanchard almost bit his tongue at the slip. "You mean there have been others here? Enemies, perhaps?"

"It looks as though others have been here," he admitted.

Cooley had counted on being a long way from anyone during his summer of exploration. Blanchard had already satisfied himself on one point. Cooley's visitors at least were not Indians. But that was not reassuring.

Less than a mile beyond, half an hour later, where a massive outthrust of rock jutted out like a roof, they found Cooley. He lay under the partial shelter, bewhiskered and disheveled, partly covered by a blanket, sprawled as if asleep.

Jumping from his horse, Blanchard hurried forward. Mavis, after a searching glance from one to the other, was at his heels, her face strained but uncertain.

"Is—this is my father?" Not having seen him over a long span of years, her uncertainty was understandable.

At Blanchard's nod, she dropped to her knees, catching a limp hand between her own, peering at the colorless face. But she waited while Blanchard made a swift but comprehensive examination, her eyes imploring. The hand he tested in turn was not stiff, though it was scarcely warm. Cooley was alive, but the indications were far from good.

Blanchard discovered no wound or outwardly serious hurt, but his friend's near-comatose condition spoke for itself. There were more signs of a camp of sorts at this spot, but he could see no supplies or articles necessary for survival.

"He's alive," he answered the unspoken question. "My guess is that he's lain unconscious for quite a while. The first thing's to get him warm. I'll unpack our supplies, then build a fire. After that, if we can fix a broth and get a few swallows down him, for a beginning . . ."

"I'll manage that," Mavis agreed, and set to work with a quiet efficiency. A closer look around showed a few discarded, useless articles in the grass and brush. Blanchard's lips tightened with understanding. They had been pawed over, apparently in a search for booty. The disorder, like the condition of her father, appalled Mavis.

"Can you tell what has happened?" she asked.

"Those others have been here," Blanchard conceded. "Enemies, almost certainly. They apparently ransacked everything. Then—and this is just a guess—they must have thought he was dead, and left him."

"You mean, they were after whatever he had found—the strike they thought he'd made?"

"They must have known, or at least had a strong belief that he had found something."

He did not amplify, nor did she question, but almost certainly they had tried to force him to reveal the location. The brief message that Cooley had managed to write and dispatch was partly explained, though there was much at which they could only guess. Blanchard's own hunch, the conviction of trouble that had oppressed them both, was grimly verified.

Here was the starkness of the primitive, the elemental savagery that had been the only law in this land since the beginning of time. In actual miles, settlements were not too distant, and change was on the way. But here they were beyond the law, and the elemental nature of man had not altered.

With a fire blazing briskly, Blanchard found water at a spring not far off and set a pan to heat, then opened up their supplies, alert against surprise. The smoke might be seen, but Cooley's condition rendered a fire imperative. Mavis prepared a sort of soup and set it to simmer, then bathed Cooley's face with warm water, cleaning away grime and traces of dried blood.

Working with the pack, Blanchard remembered the bottles of whiskey, but decided against them for the moment. He had brought them along chiefly because Cooley enjoyed a nip on occasion and would be especially pleased after a long, dry summer. A swallow or so might help, but it might be as well to try the broth first.

He came up from his haunches, swiftly alert, and Mavis checked stirring the broth, catching his strained watchfulness. Almost at once it was explained as she heard another sound, one familiar yet somehow alien. Their own ponies were close by, standing virtually motionless, but the clop-clop of hoofs was drawing nearer.

In so restricted a space, hemmed by hills and trees, there was nothing to see. Then the sound was momentarily shut away.

"It sounds as though that other bunch is coming back," Blanchard whispered, but in the harshness of his tone was a growing suspicion. Judging by such sign as they had come upon, those others had had no horses.

Yet the odds that any who might be dropping in upon them at this particular time and in such fashion would be friendly was even more unlikely.

And whoever was coming, they almost certainly were riding.

9

The riders swung into sight, urging jaded animals to a faster pace, and Blanchard expelled a sigh of resignation and frustration. Despite his best efforts, all his skill at hiding a trail, even avoiding the telltale sound of a rifle when the grizzly and the bull had intervened, Gentleman Jim Kearns and his inveterate shadows had caught up.

They had pack animals of their own, and they were peering avidly ahead, eager as wolves at the kill. Gentleman Jim somehow managed to give the impression of spruceness and jauntiness under almost all circumstances. Aided by an easy grin and a rough good nature, he gave an initial aura of reassurance. But a fox in a hen yard seemed also to smile.

Cloud was massive in the saddle, stolid, belying the sharpness of eyes and keenness of mind that could read sign, following even a cold trail. Silverman, gangly and loose-jointed, was the least predictable, the most impulsive and in some ways most dangerous.

A gloating triumph was quickly smoothed as

Kearns saw that they were observed in turn. Their attention strayed between doubt and question from Mavis and Blanchard to the unstirring figure of Cooley. Kneeling beside him, Mavis's face had gone white.

"Well, well, if this isn't a surprise, finding you folks way off here!" Kearns was rarely at a loss for words. Blanchard confirmed what he had expected, that all three were well armed.

"I hope there's nothing seriously wrong with your father, Miss Cooley," Kearns went on. "As an old friend, I've worried about him for some time, and when I got to thinking it over, we came along to see if we could be of help." He nodded affably to Blanchard. "This is wild country for a man alone."

"That was the way he wanted it," Blanchard returned pointedly. "As to it being a surprise, after trailing us as you've done—" He shrugged.

Somehow they had managed to follow Blanchard's carefully concealed trail, so sure of themselves as well as eager that they had wasted no time in making their presence known, with the clear intention of taking control. What they had not counted on was that others had been before them. So unknown a threat might exert a restraining influence, at least for a while.

"Trailing you? Surely you don't suppose—" Kearns looked hurt. "We had been planning a trip this way for some time, and everything considered, it seemed to be the proper one. As to tracking a man of your skill, if you didn't want to be followed, what chance would we have had?"

Silverman suppressed a snort of laughter. Blanchard was not deceived. This protestation was for Mavis's benefit, though he doubted that she was fooled. Kearns had managed to make use of her at the start, but the role of old family friend was already wearing thin.

"But you caught up," Blanchard reminded dryly.

"Pure chance, or luck," Kearns insisted. "We heard a bawling and bellowing, which aroused our curiosity, and upon investigating, came upon the dead bear and bull. That must have been an epic battle. With the hoofmarks of several horses leading away from the vicinity, we deduced that it must be you—and of course, under the circumstances, we followed."

That explained it. They had been close enough to hear, but had probably been as bewildered as Blanchard had intended. The clash of the behemoths had been unforeseen, beyond his control, undoing all his efforts to hide their trail. That it had not been his fault was not much consolation.

"But what's wrong with Jeb?" Kearns went on. His darting glances had told him the same story, that several people from a third group had been there ahead of them. Almost certainly they had been after the same prize: knowledge of the strike that Cooley had written about. If they had succeeded in extracting the secret from him . . .

Or even if they had not, but if they had left him so seriously injured he would not recover . . .

"You can see how he's been treated," Blanchard said grimly. "But we just got here. He's unconscious—what looks like a sort of coma. I hope we can bring him out of it."

Dismayed apprehension was forcing an alteration in their plans. Clearly they had intended to take charge, but cooperation, at least for a while, seemed to be called for.

"What can we do?" Kearns asked. "I'm terribly sorry about this, Miss Cooley, believe me. We've *got* to do something."

"The first thing, of course, is get him warm and get more broth down him," Blanchard pointed out. "But what he really needs is to see a doctor, and the sooner the better. That is going to be a lot of work, and it will need all of us to manage properly. We'll need to start back, first thing in the morning."

His acquiescence took Kearns off-guard. This was a game, and the stakes were high. Blanchard was calling his bluff. Having come up with Cooley, locating the country where he had spent the summer, the trio's overriding interest was to find what he had discovered, then jump his claim. To turn back at once, without even a chance to look around, fitted no part of their plan.

Kearns stared thoughtfully at the sick man, while Mavis busied herself with the broth.

"Aren't you jumping to conclusions?" he protested. "I'll go along with you that he would be better under a doctor's care, Blanchard, but I'm not at all sure that it would be the right thing to move him. At best, it would be a long and tiring ordeal—maybe too exhausting. We don't know just how badly he is hurt, and we can't risk making it worse."

"You may be right," Blanchard conceded. "But since you agree that he needs a doctor, one of you can head back and bring one."

"That's just as unrealistic," Kearns contradicted. "Even if we could persuade a doctor to make the trip here, reaching and bringing him would take at least another couple of weeks. By that time, he'll either be better, or—well, it's up to us to do the best we can for him," he ended. "We have to face facts."

Such sparring merely delayed a showdown, but it removed any doubts that Mavis might have entertained as to the real purpose of the trio. Blanchard had never had any. Kearns was serving notice that business had to come first, and all else, even a man's life, was secondary. That he was confident of having the upper hand, being in a position to dictate terms, was equally obvious.

Blanchard shrugged, then turned to assist Mavis as she set about to spoon some of the broth to her father. Her solicitude was obvious, though to her he was a virtual stranger. They managed to get a few swallows down his throat, though he did not swallow easily. Her eyes questioned Blanchard. For the moment there was nothing that he could say or do.

Cooley's brief, rather cryptic message by pigeon had made it clear that he had found what he had searched for, and the news, obviously, was no longer a secret. Already the vultures were gathering. A second and unknown bunch had tried to wrest his secret from him, probably without success. Even without knowing Cooley's stubbornness, the sign was easy to read. Attempting to force Cooley to talk, someone had lost his temper and slugged or mistreated him to the point of lingering unconsciousness. Frustrated, probably thinking him dead, they had set out on a search—one that would probably leave them still more frustrated and desperate.

And that would probably bring them back, on the long chance of his survival or of finding some clue they had overlooked.

Such a return would force another showdown, in which Kearns would be an uncertain ally, ready to join with the others if he saw any hope of profit in such an alliance.

For the present, Kearns would be as helpful as possible, since Cooley's secret could only be discovered with Cooley's help. But, if he was restored to normal health, Cooley might still be unwilling to cooperate. It was an unpromising situation, with Kearns refusing to divide and weaken his own force.

Compounding the human element, winter was not far off.

Back at Cooley's ranch a week before, the heat of an Indian summer day had been too great for comfort. But the geese had been on their trek down from the north, and here, close up to the border with Canada, winter could strike sudden and hard. To be caught by increasing storms could be fatal.

Mavis finally gave up the attempt with the broth. Her mounting uneasiness was plain.

"I think just as Mr. Blanchard does—that we should start back without delay," she asserted. "Couldn't you men rig some sort of a litter or sled—

something to be pulled by a couple of the horses?"

"You mean, such as the Indians sometimes use?" Kearns shook his head. "I was once *assisted* in that fashion, with the best of intentions, but I still have a vivid memory of the jolting, endless miles. I'd take my chances without, any time."

Mavis's temper flared.

"You've been protesting all along that all you wanted was to try and help him—and me. Well, if you really want to, then it's for me, and Mr. Blanchard, as his friend and partner, to decide. If you will assist us, then let's make ready and get an early start. If you don't want to, just say so, and we'll do it ourselves."

Silverman tittered. Kearns shot him a black look, and his temper, always on short leash, frayed dangerously.

"You just don't know what you're talking about, girl," he snapped. "It would be the worst possible thing—"

Spots of color blazed in Mavis's cheeks as she confronted him.

"It sounds to me as though you didn't want to help—or at least that you don't want him out from here. Is that it?"

Kearns managed a placating smile.

"Now, now, Miss Mavis, you're jumping to conclusions—"

"Is that it? You're actually here because you think he's made a strike, and you're hoping to steal it."

Again, Silverman tittered. Kearns swung angrily.

"Shut up, you fool!" As he turned again to Mavis,

his hand hovered close to his gun, his attention warily on Blanchard. Cloud, for all his seeming stolidity, had slipped to the side, in a flanking position should trouble erupt.

"How can you say such things, Miss Mavis? Why should we even think that he'd made a strike—"

He broke off, realizing his blunder. Her lip curled.

"So you're a liar as well as a would-be thief, Mr. Kearns? You knew he had found something, and now you hope to stop us from getting him out, even to save his life, just so that you can find what it is, and where—"

She checked at Silverman's recurrent cackle, grimness in the faces of all three. Belatedly she was recognizing not only how badly off was her father but that they were isolated in a remote wilderness.

"That's about the size of the matter," Kearns admitted, suddenly bland. "Which leaves some things to talk over and settle before anybody goes anywhere. As—"

The tautness of overstrained nerves was common to both sides. Kearns jumped in concert with Mavis at the sudden blast of a heavy-caliber gun, its thunder coming almost from under their ears.

10

Kearns swung angrily, doubly enraged at being caught off-guard by one of his own companions. Cloud was returning the heavy forty-five to its holster while a big steer, outlined against the hillcrest a short distance above, swayed before it suddenly collapsed, toppling and sliding half the distance to the bottom. Whether chance or curiosity had brought it there at such a moment, Cloud had been quick to recognize the opportunity and take advantage.

The wide span of horns, coupled with the size, testified to the age of the steer. That it should be dropped by a single shot told something of Cloud's prowess with a gun.

"What the devil do you think you're about?" Kearns demanded, but the heavy-set man only gestured.

"Meat," he explained, then added, "beef will make better broth for Cooley."

That was so clearly evident on both counts that Kearns's temper cooled. Blanchard, initially as startled as any, noticed something that seemed to have escaped the others. Still plain on the big steer's side was a sprawling Double Diamond—Slade Tatum's brand.

This meat would be lean and tough, since the steer was one of the survivors of the original herd. Finding it there was additional proof that the herd had been brought to this remote section, then left to shift for themselves. It was also an indication that Cooley had founded his hunch on something more substantial than guesswork, though its significance still eluded Blanchard.

Giving over discussion for the moment, they lost no time in butchering the steer, Blanchard taking charge when it became clear that the others hardly knew how to proceed. Presently Mavis was broiling steaks, along with fixing a fresh broth. On that point at least there was no disagreement. The interlopers were as anxious as Mavis that her father be restored to health, at least enough to talk, so that hopefully he might disclose the location of his strike.

Blanchard went along with the tacit truce. He still had his gun, but the odds against a forced showdown were not to his liking. Jeb was dangerously ill, and having brought her here, though at her demand, Jeb's girl was his responsibility.

Kearns, increasingly confident that he had the situation under control, still was not satisfied, but must wait to press the issue.

Biscuits hot from a Dutch oven, coffee, and the steaks made a satisfying meal. Kearns resumed the interrupted discussion.

"We may as well come to an understanding," he said smoothly. "That can save trouble. It's sure too bad that Cooley is unable for the time being to assist us—"

"Just how could he do that?" Mavis demanded.

"It's his strike I'm referring to," Kearns admitted. "Judging by the shape he's in, others have been unable to find it, so it's doubtful that we could do any better. And he certainly wanted you to have it, Miss Mavis—"

"I'm sure he did," she granted. "If you're so anxious to help me, and so disinterested, it will be easy enough to prove. We can draw up a paper, making it clear that Mr. Blanchard, as his partner, and I, as his daughter, are the sole and rightful heirs to anything that may be found. That was what you wanted, as I understand."

Kearns looked hurt. "Is such a paper necessary between friends? Can't you trust us?"

"I've always been told that it's better for everyone to have such matters down in writing. If you mean what you say—"

"It seems to me that this is a question of mutual cooperation for common survival," Kearns flared. "Under the circumstances, I would think that a partnership would be only fair."

"Meaning that you are here only to steal his strike? First you'd jump his claim, then under the name of a partnership force us to give such robbery a semblance of legality!"

Silverman chortled. Well fed, confident of the outcome, he was enjoying himself.

"She ain't easy to fool, Jim," he said.

"But you're a fool," Kearns returned bitterly. "You overlook one obvious fact, Mavis, which is that we have control here. Though it appears that others have muscled in ahead of us, so we need to take common action to protect our mutual interests."

Just who those others might be worried him as much as the other aspects. He went on earnestly. "Your father seemed pretty sure that he had made another really big strike. Knowing him, I'm willing to go along with his judgment, so if he's right, there should be enough for all of us, without quarreling over the spoils. On that basis, we're willing to cooperate."

Mavis remained forthright. "And if we refuse?"

His shrug was elaborate. "That would be too bad. In fact, I'd consider it as very ill advised. Eh, Blanchard?"

"That would remain to be seen." Mavis had made a complete turnaround, and he admired her spirit. "Aren't you taking a lot for granted?"

"For instance?"

"You keep talking of a strike, and by that I suppose you mean gold. But when Cooley and I discussed his trip back here, he never said a word about gold, or what he really hoped to find."

Kearns was impatient. "What else could it be? You're just trying to throw dirt into our eyes. What it comes down to is to accept reality now, or fight it. Which would be a bad mistake."

Mavis turned to Blanchard, torn between anger and despair. "Do we have to put up with this?"

"You're as stubborn as your dad," Kearns retorted, not without admiration. "I've been trying to make you understand that we are in control now. Just to avoid any trouble, Blanchard, you'd better give me your gun."

Blanchard handed it over. He had hoped to delay the showdown, but the odds for resistance were suicidal, and Cloud, at least, was eager for an excuse to kill. And once he was out of the way...

"You win this trick, Kearns," he said. "But it's a dangerous game."

Kearns nodded, with no further pretense. "High stakes are always dangerous." He shrugged. "And I've a notion that this is the biggest game I've ever sat in, one worth gambling for. I'm in it to win. I hope we understand each other."

He had gone too far to back down. Having shown his intention, it was all or nothing.

As full understanding was forced on Mavis, she was close to tears. Back in town, Kearns had acted a part, playing it convincingly. The reality left her appalled.

"Oh, Harry, I'm sorry to have been such a dupe, such a—a fool," she gasped. "I—I guess I've spoiled everything, for everyone, for being so trusting and believing the things he told me. Right away, I rushed to you—just in time to stop you from getting away—and I made all those ridiculous charges! Y-you must hate me—"

Silverman tittered. Kearns glared at him, furious.

"I reckon he's a long way from hating you, Miss Mavis," he cut in. "And don't blame yourself too much. You didn't understand, and though you were helpful, I'd have managed. When that first carrier pigeon was caught by a hawk, we were lucky enough to see and make a guess, and Cloud shot the hawk. Only the message was too torn to mean much. But we got the next one, so what you did didn't much matter."

Until now, busy with gathering firewood and other chores, Cloud had listened in silence. Now he interrupted impatiently. Whatever Kearns intended, he and Silverman clearly looked on themselves as full partners in the venture, not hired hands.

"Are we going to gab all day?" he demanded. "There're things to do."

"All this trouble comes from my being headstrong as well as ignorant," Mavis said contritely. "Since Dad has always trusted you, Harry, from now on I'll do the same. You understand what is involved, so use your own judgment."

"Now, that's showing good sense." Kearns was only half mocking. "I hope yours will match, Blanchard."

"You seem to hold the trumps," Blanchard conceded. "What are your terms?"

Kearns did not even glance at his helpers. "Cooperation and partnership. What else?"

"Partnership?" Silverman protested. "Are you crazy . . . ?"

"I'm running this," Kearns snapped, and Cloud, with surer insight, said nothing. Blanchard hesitated. For the moment it might be better to let things ride, since Kearns, even if pinned down, was as slippery as quicksilver. On the other hand, the offer might hold a faint chance.

"Any deal or partnership will be empty unless we get Cooley to a doctor. He knows where the strike is—and he's the only one who does."

"Are we back to that?" Kearns too-ready tongue betrayed him. "Once out of this country, you'd be in control, not us. We have it now, and we'll keep it. Until we find the strike and have it staked, we stay."

11

Kearns swung away, a gesture of finality. Mavis remained on the verge of tears.

"I was such a stupid little fool," she said bitterly. "If I'd only been frank with you at the start, none of this would have happened. Now I've spoiled everything."

"It wasn't your fault—or at least, no more than mine," Blanchard returned. "You didn't know him. I did, and I underestimated his capabilities. But it isn't all one-sided, by any means."

Momentarily they were alone, with a chance to talk. She was deeply troubled.

"It's generous of you to say that, but I've gotten us into a real mess. What about Dad? We can't get out with him. And if we have to stay, and he gets better—"

Blanchard shared her fear. They both wanted Cooley to recover, but his return to consciousness would involve worse dangers, not alone for him but for them.

"He's been rather badly used, but he's about as tough as they come, and proud of it. With good care, I think he'll make it. That comes first. We can take only one step at a time, the way things are."

"Of course." She spoke not merely with resigned acceptance, but with a courage Blanchard was coming to admire. "But just how bad is it—the overall situation?"

"Bad enough," he admitted. "If things work out as they hope, and they could get hold of a rich claim, I think Kearns would give us a small share, if he were assured that we would keep still, not prefer charges against them. The trouble is that all of them have records—and after going this far, they'll keep on, to whatever lengths they figure are necessary to win."

Her face whitened with understanding.

"But you have friends—and there's Dad's ranch crew. Not many know about me, or would remember. But *you* can't just disappear. If you don't return, surely there would be a search, with the law called in—"

"The ranch and the law are a long way off. Back in here, winter will come ahead of anything like that. By spring, the snows will have covered . . . who knows? Kearns knows the odds and is counting on them, gambling for the breaks."

Her headshake was still half incredulous. "He seemed such a fine man! His letters, everything. He talks and acts like a gentleman—most of the time."

"He's an actor, not a gentleman, though he can act like one when it suits him—and when he's sober. Let's hope they have no liquor along." He started with sudden remembrance of his own momentarily forgotten flasks. "You keep an eye on Cooley. There're some things I need to do."

With night almost at hand, Kearns was turning almost regretfully from the charade that he so clearly enjoyed to necessary preparations to insure continuing control. It was sheer luck that the store of whiskey had gone undiscovered, but that could hardly last.

Cloud was unpacking their own laden pony, Kearns and Silverman deciding on various matters. If it should occur to them that he might have brought even a single bottle...

At all costs, the whiskey had to be kept from them. Blanchard knew how they reacted to liquor.

He moved to join in the work, opening up his own pack, carting supplies toward the overhang, tossing the tent to one side. He could set it up later. With the bottles wrapped in a blanket, he hesitated. How to get rid of them, almost under their noses, was the problem.

He would cheerfully present them to the three as a gesture of goodwill, but he dared not take the risk. Aware of their own weakness, apparently they had not brought any, since resultant quarrels could turn ugly.

One course would be to pour it out, or smash the bottles. But that would probably attract attention, as the fumes spread, and bring a bitter reaction. The safest way for the moment was to cache the bottles until a better opportunity was presented.

Noticing him, Cloud brusquely ordered him to

bring the supplies to a common pile, and Blanchard complied. Then he turned to pitch the tent, cutting a fresh supply of spruce boughs for a mattress. On their good behavior for the moment, no one objected. It was to their interest that Mavis give her father the best of care, so that if possible he would regain strength and consciousness.

A further feeding of strong beef broth was being swallowed almost eagerly, and Jeb seemed to hover at the verge of returning reason. A touch of color returned to his face, his breathing was more even.

His recovery would bring fresh problems, helping to even the odds. But for the present, everyone had to play for the breaks.

Morning brought no outward change in Cooley's condition, and since it was clear that Cooley could be of no help, at least for some time to come, and with time growing short as winter threatened, the trio set out to explore; that a search was likely to prove hopeless, where others had failed with much more time, did not stop them. On the verge of desperation, devil-driven, only one appetite was greater than the lust for gold.

Blanchard, caring for the horses—in their eagerness the others had even forgotten their own animals—was shifting a picket rope when a muffled scream brought him on a run. Cloud had returned, slipping away from the others. Darting out suddenly from the brush, he had surprised Mavis, now struggling wildly in his arms.

"Don't be a fool, girl," he advised roughly. "Ain't nothin' or nobody can stop me from takin' what I want. If you're countin' on Blanchard, it'd take half a dozen of him—"

That his boast was only half true, even in his own ears, was shown as he glimpsed Blanchard and swung to meet his rush, flinging Mavis aside as only an encumbrance. She fell, sprawling, to lie panting and disheveled.

Blanchard had not paused even to find a club. In the wild madness that gripped him, he wanted only to come to grips with an adversary, and Cloud, equally anxious, disdained to grab for his revolver. The next instant Blanchard was upon him.

Fury did not rob him of caution. Cloud's boast was not an idle one, but was founded on experience. His grip on an enemy was hardly less devastating than the hug of a grizzly. He had cracked men's ribs, driving the breath from their body, flinging them to earth, completing the job in lumberjack fashion, boots smashing, pounding like piledrivers.

Running headlong, Blanchard launched himself in a high leap. Cloud tried to jump aside, an instant too late. Blanchard was literally all over him, legs scissoring in a knifing grip about the big man's waist, his hands finding the bull-thick neck, closing in a throttling embrace.

Surprise coursed through Blanchard as Cloud remained on his feet, not driven down by such an assault. Again he was like the grizzly, but the grip of Blanchard's legs prisoned his arms. He sought frantically to tear them loose, to slug or grasp in turn, as fingers as choking as the jaws of a trap shut off his wind.

Staggering, Cloud's legs gave way, and they crashed down together, Blanchard uppermost. That Cloud's head cracked hard on a rock was a mischance. Feeling him go limp, Blanchard released his hold, scrambling for the dropped revolver. But it had fallen to the side, and Kearns's sardonic tones were implicit with threat.

"Leave it lay! Not that I blame you—but you're too riled to trust with a gun." His own was trained on Blanchard at point-blank range.

12

The trio might work together where booty was at stake, but there was no trust between them. Cloud had circled off by himself, and Kearns, discovering it and strongly suspicious of what he might be about, had lost no time in swinging back. Recriminations followed as Cloud sat up groggily.

"You got only what was coming to you," Kearns growled. "Trying to ruin everything! You'll keep in mind, mister, that this was my idea and that I'm running the show! I'll have no more such acting up." He turned solicitously to Mavis, still white-faced and shaken. "I'm mighty sorry. It won't happen again. You tell me if he even tries to step out of line, and I'll currycomb him."

Kearns was a strange mixture, and unpredictable. Stubborn to the point of mulishness, he had clearly given up any hope of stumbling upon Jeb Cooley's strike in such time as remained before winter shut away all leads, and was now pinning his hopes on Cooley's recovery and cooperation, however unwilling.

Events had gotten out of hand. Kearns had hoped to convince Mavis that he was a long-time friend of her father's, anxious to help both of them. Now, along with his helpers, he was revealed for what he was, and with the law as with Mavis and Blanchard, they had already passed the point of no return.

Silverman was unpredictable, Cloud coldly vicious. And if those others, who had tried to force Cooley's secret from him and then left him for dead, should return . . .

Cloud sulked, keeping to himself. Reassured by Kearns's presence, Blanchard explored the vicinity of the camp, making sure that the horses were cared for. The sunshine of the past several days had given way to clouds, the threat of storm.

Mavis remained close to her father, whose condition showed no change, though she managed to get a few swallows of broth down his throat. After the initial shock of Cloud's brutality, she was composed, coldly aloof, except with Blanchard.

"Isn't there anything we can do?" she asked, then amended that. "*Is* there anything? We must—somehow."

"We will," Blanchard assured her. "Right now, they're playing for the breaks, but we hold a few trumps in this game. And we'll play our cards to the limit—"

He broke off at a sudden babel of voices, rising, then as quickly muted. Silverman had built up a big fire, partly for cooking, largely against the closing darkness at day's end. Cloud sat, a shadowy, substantial figure at the far rim of the firelight, a rifle at the ready.

Opposite, on the far side, were a cluster of newcomers, who almost certainly would be those who had visited Cooley before. They had halted at sight of others, with a wary unease. Their excited exclamations at discovering a fire sprang from hope as well as belief that Cooley had recovered enough to get one started.

Their return suggested that their search for his strike had failed. Blanchard made out another trio of men in the foreground, of a matching toughness in appearance. Two others, huddling uncertainly behind them, were more surprising.

One was a woman, wearing a heavy, shapeless coat, yet despite it looking somehow frail and small. Clinging to her hand, clearly sharing her unease rather than the excitement of the men, was a child, who might be eight or ten. The same wary, pinched look was common to both faces, reflected in the fireglow on the young, yet too-old face.

One of the newcomers carried a rifle, the only one that Blanchard could see, but it was matched by an axe and club in the grasp of his companions. Clad more in skins than modern garments, they were like a remnant of a lost tribe, suggesting survivors of a stone age, just emerging from the long dusk.

There was no sign of Kearns or Silverman, which perhaps encouraged the newcomers in their assessment of the situation. Seeing the woman and child, Blanchard felt a surge of sympathy. But the men were dangerous. The way they had treated Cooley was a grim warning.

Cloud challenged, a ripple of firelight reflected from the leveled barrel of his rifle. "What do you want?"

The other rifleman was of a matching bulk and solidity.

"Let's just turn that question around," he growled. "Who might you be, and what the hell are you doing here?" A raging undertone like the grizzly's growl echoed in his voice.

Cloud, always slow-witted, was striving to adjust to the surprise. His need to reply was postponed as Kearns and Silverman came circling out from the gloom to the left, taking their stands on either side of Cloud. Both were looking along leveled revolvers. At their materialization the big man's eyes batted, then, with incredulous recognition, his head thrust forward, again like the grizzly's.

"Jim Kearns! Gentleman Jim!" He spat with undisguised contempt. "I might a knowed! I thought I smelled skunk."

Kearns's face went a deeper red than the firelight justified, but he was adroit at hiding his own surprise. He shrugged.

"When it comes to that, you've the nose of a wolf when there's a carcass to pick! The only thing that really surprises me is that you're still alive, Lundy. I figured somebody would have lynched you long before this."

With head thrust forward after the manner of a

vulture, Lundy swallowed. His resemblance to the carrion bird was unpleasantly apparent.

"I'll be around to watch when *you're* kickin' in a noose, Kearns. Unless I have to shoot you first. Which by rights I ought to do right now!"

Kearns sounded amused. He had assessed the situation and adjusted to the altered reality.

"Don't try to bluff me," he said contemptuously. "I know you too well. But we'd be crazy to fight among ourselves when there's no need. Since we're all here, this should be a great party. We're all looking for what Cooley turned up, which has to be somewhere hereabouts. Knowing him, it's a deadwood cinch that there'll be plenty for everybody. So let's be reasonable about it. Working together is your only chance. For it's easy to see that the methods you used, working Cooley over to try and make him talk, got you nowhere."

"You mean him?" Apparently they had been unaware of Cooley's name, for Lundy jerked a thumb toward the unconscious prospector. His attention was wandering, his eyes lingering on Mavis, as she stood protectively close to her father. Reluctantly he brought his gaze back to Kearns, then nodded.

"He turned stubborn," he explained.

Silverman gave a sudden cackle, drawing a scowl from both leaders. Kearns's question was more to needle than in search of information.

"Did he tell you anything?" he challenged.

Unexpectedly, vindictively, the child piped up from the shadows. "He told them to go to hell!"

Lundy spun about, snarling, but checked as Kearns's laughter boomed.

"That's about what I'd expect," Kearns observed. "Who was it said, out of the mouths of babes? Well, you should have known what to expect. Cooley can be as rough and tough as the occasion calls for. But you're too dumb to learn. You're back, on the off-chance that he might still be alive. Pretty late to think about that, but it's lucky we got here in time to take a hand. You've found nothing, hunting by yourselves, and after looking this country over, it's easy to see why."

Abruptly he became friendly, almost cordial.

"From the smell, the little lady's roasting some beef, and I'm certain we'd fare no better at Delmonico's." As his reference was met with blank incomprehension, he went on. "So, since supper's ready, let's eat. We can make medicine afterward."

Suspicious and hostile both by instinct and knowledge of his adversary, Lundy hesitated. Then the aroma of the roasting beef proved too tempting.

"Suits me. You mean nobody starts nothin'—not till we eat and talk?"

"Your grasp of the situation encompasses every detail." Kearns holstered his gun, and the others, after a moment, followed his example. Cloud, at Kearns's nod, turned to assist Mavis in dishing up the supper. Making use of the supplies that both groups had brought in, she had contrived a tasty repast. They squatted about in small, mutually distrustful groups, Mavis keeping close to her father, Blanchard half cloaked by the darkness behind. Lundy gnawed voraciously at a beef bone, much as a medieval squire at his own board. Curiosity overcame his still-smouldering resentment.

"Where'd you come from, Kearns? And how'n blazes did you find your way in here?"

Kearns tossed a picked bone at the fire. "Simple. We trailed Blanchard and Cooley's daughter, when they headed this way to help him."

The glibness of his explanation left the newcomers uncertain. Taking advantage of their bewilderment, Kearns asked an apparently careless question of his own.

"I take it you've been spending the summer back in here, doing some prospecting on your own?"

Lundy nodded. "Sort of. We just sort of drifted this way, as you might say."

The others listened but remained carefully silent. Such glimpses as Blanchard could obtain of the other woman and child, in the flickering fireglow, revealed nothing. Along with Kearns, he had a fairly clear understanding.

Lundy, like Kearns, was an outlaw by inclination, preferring to live by his wits rather than a steady job, never realizing that he worked harder for smaller and less certain returns. Like Kearns, he had his followers, and clearly they lived like nomads, hunting, fishing and trapping, with a bit of prospecting on the side. If their luck could be improved by jumping another man's claim, they were as ready as Kearns for such a course, differing only in directness and savagery.

Discovering Cooley and guessing what he was about, they had probably watched him for days or weeks. Finally, losing patience, they had moved to attack, undoubtedly striking without warning. Whether or not they had found gold in his possession, at least they were convinced that he had made a strike. Failing to force the secret from him, they had explored again, then, increasingly frustrated, had returned in the hope of finding some clue around his camp.

Lundy's eyes kept returning to Mavis. "Who'd you say she is?" he asked.

"I told you. She's Cooley's daughter. And while we're about it, this is Harry Blanchard, who helped Cooley come here last spring and has returned to give him a hand. And now, let's get a few things straight, right from the start. No rough stuff. You tried that, and it didn't work. Another thing—there's a storm on the way, which means that winter can close in on us any time. Which doesn't leave much time, and none to waste. Our best chance—and likely our only one—is to all work together. And that means, if we can be that lucky, to get Cooley well again."

His outline sounded reasonable, but distrust was inherent in Lundy's nature; moreover, he knew Kearns.

"Blast you, Kearns, don't try to tell me how to do things. You act like you figured you were the boss—"

"All I'm suggesting is that we work together," Kearns reminded. "But somebody has to be in charge."

Lundy helped himself to more meat, not bothering

to reply. With the closing night and approaching storm, the air held an increasing bite. Blanchard noticed that the woman and child kept as far as possible from Lundy, as close to Mavis and himself as they dared come without exciting a reprimand.

The little girl, in the grip of unusual excitement, had voiced defiance for Lundy, but it was easy to see that all the others were afraid of him, cowed to the point of actual terror. The furtive manner in which they watched him reminded Blanchard of a dog, wary of a cuff or kick.

Their return was certainly no improvement. Both groups were at or beyond the fringes of the law, suspicious of each other, but basically with a mutual purpose—to find Jeb Cooley's strike and have it for themselves.

Jeb's condition was a worry, one more complication in a situation that was increasingly complicated. There might be one possibility, if he could find a way to work it: to work on their greed and jealousy, and set them at each other's throats.

Blanchard started at his name, spoken softly but sounding unexpectedly loud in a moment of sudden hush.

"You don't remember me, do you, Mr. Blanchard?"

It was the woman who had spoken, from the shadows just behind.

13

The words had been intended for Blanchard's ears alone, but the bad luck that dogged them increasingly had left them suddenly audible, instead of covered by talk and a clatter of tinware. Her face flamed doubly red against the glow of the fire as Lundy swung about, then burst into a mocking guffaw.

"What, Eve?" he roared. "Don't tell me you two know each other? But I reckon you do. *Now* I see it!" The sudden mockery in his voice was half triumph, part vindictive.

"You wouldn't be telling us that this is your old sweetheart, the fine dude that shined around you when you was just a slip of a girl at the mission! Only after that he didn't figure that a half-breed gal like you was good enough for the likes of him! But of course it has to be him, with that name, and you rememberin' him! And he turns up at a time like this."

The woman shrank before Lundy's coarse taunting, dismayed at being heard and the sudden wild triumph in the outlaw's eyes. The others were listening with equal surprise, Mavis with a look of bewilderment as she looked from one to another, but mostly at Blanchard. He was as astonished as any.

His initial incredulity gave way to dawning recognition as he heard the name and saw the flush suffusing the girl's face. Already it had been a day of surprises, but this was easily the culmination. This girl had been Eve Porter when he had known her nearly a decade before. A decade in which he had lost all trace of her.

He had been rodding a trail herd, all the way up from Texas then. With the end of the trail in sight, a mishap had laid him low, as his horse had fallen and rolled on him.

But his luck had held, not only in surviving, but in that a small mission and school for the Indians had been close at hand. They had found him, and over a period of months, the sisters had nursed him back to health.

Eve had been one of the pupils at the school—a great-eyed waif whom the sisters had also taken in, a bit of flotsam spilled out from the migrations of westward-rolling wagons. She had been pretty and eager, always helpful, somewhat awed by the cowboy and the world from which he came. Thinking back, Blanchard remembered how lonely he had been amid surroundings kindly but strange—everyone else had spoken French or Indian. Only Eve had understood English, and she had served as an interpreter.

They had been good friends, and that was all. That the shyly budding child might have viewed him in a romantic light had not occurred to him. She had simply been a helpful friend, her position in some aspects paralleling his own. In the years since, he had occasionally remembered, wondering what they had held for her, hoping that fate had been kind.

Here was the answer. Clearly, it had not.

The years, and the hardships of the life to which she had been subjected, had changed her. They had almost but not quite snuffed out such hope and much of the beauty that had bloomed so briefly at the rim of the prairie. The child, of course, was hers, just as Lundy, equally clearly, was her man.

In that there was nothing very unusual, though Blanchard realized that he had hoped for better where she was concerned. But this was the pattern of the frontier, or for that matter, of humanity everywhere. Women had a way of giving their loyalty to worthless men, then following wild and lonely lands.

The blaze of color that swept her face at Lundy's jibe was proof that she retained some of the qualities Blanchard had found attractive, along with a remembrance of the sisters' teachings. With it was the impression of a hound that had been kicked about until it expected nothing better. The momentary excitement faded from her eyes.

"Why, Eve," Blanchard returned, and swung to face her, "you—I didn't expect to find you here."

"I'm sure it's a surprise for both of us." Her voice was small, and she clearly regretted having made herself known. "It—since you were here, I wanted to say hello. It—it's been a long while."

"Not long enough for you though, I'll bet," Lundy gibed again, glaring now at Blanchard. "You've traveled other trails, ain't you? And got yourself a new sweetheart—at least till it's handy to run off and leave her in the lurch, too!"

Blanchard swung in sudden fury at what Lundy was implying. There was hate in this man, fostered and fermented by failure, and he caught the note of wild jealousy, of resentments that had smouldered and festered a long while. Somehow, perhaps by chance remarks heard at the mission or wormed from Eve herself in unguarded moments, Lundy had learned of that summer's friendship. Undoubtedly, Eve had regretted bitterly taking up with such a man, being tormented into speaking of Blanchard, perhaps boasting that she had once had a more desirable lover.

The effect on Lundy had been less than happy. Jealously resentful, he had made her as much a drudge as most women became with men like himself, taking out his spite on her, then, observing how it bothered her, on the child. Now he had a fresh outlet for his vindictiveness.

"Bridle your tongue!" Blanchard snapped. "It's a lie, and I don't take such talk from anyone."

Belatedly he remembered his own lack of a weapon, a condition Lundy had made certain of and was emboldened by. Lundy's gun was back in hand, the reflected fire-glint along its barrel matching the flare in his eyes.

"You'll take it from me!" he gritted. "I've long hankered for a chance at you, feller, and there ain't no time like the present!"

14

The gun in Lundy's hand was shifting, and it was clear to Blanchard that Kearns had no intention of intervening. Jeb Cooley was important, at least until they could wrest his secret from him, but Blanchard possessed no such value and was also a serious problem. And then, belatedly, sly as a fox at a chicken yard, Kearns's gun was also lifting, and Blanchard saw what he had in mind. To let Lundy dispose of Blanchard, then, self-righteously and before Lundy could shift aim or recover, to gun him down in turn.

Lundy was beyond reach, even for a jump; but there was something closer at hand. Blanchard kicked out, and his boot caught a blazing stick of wood from the edge of the fire, lifting, driving. The ember struck Lundy's wrist, but instead of falling caught and lodged against his revolver. Screaming, he shook it loose, but a scent akin to the branding of a calf filled the air.

Blanchard crossed the gap in a rush, and the gun came loose from Lundy's lax grip in a single twist.

But before he could shift his grip from barrel to butt and swing to face Kearns, his weapon was lined in turn. Alarm widened his eyes at the ease with which Blanchard had reversed the situation.

"Hold it," he gasped. "Both of you are fools," he added belatedly, and was himself again, righteously indignant. "What ails you, Lundy? These folks are our guests. We want no trouble."

Whether Lundy belatedly sensed what Kearns had had in mind and the narrowness of his own escape, a sullen unease was tempered by the pain of his burn. He glared like a cornered wolf.

"You're the fool," he returned. "What about my gun?"

Blanchard threw it into the thickening darkness. With Kearns's gun covering him and the extra men of both groups ready to leap like a wolf pack, there was no chance of holding on to it. For the rest of the night, at least, it would be out of the way.

"You can find it tomorrow, Lundy." He shrugged. "Better be careful if you do. A gun can be dangerous."

Lundy was growling for someone to fetch some grease to smear on his burn. Eve obeyed, working with a swift efficiency that drew no thanks in response. Sullenly Lundy returned to the interrupted meal, and after a moment the rest resumed eating as well. Tension crowded like the encroaching night.

For the moment it was an uneasy truce, but like a ruptured keg, powder had been scattered everywhere, ready to flame without warning. Somewhere, far off, a cow bawled, the sound long-drawn, lonely.

Cloud started, and faces in the reflected fireglow showed as apprehensive as if it had been the roar of a grizzly. This was the country of the lost herd.

Eve and the child ate in silence, keeping to the background, as far removed from Lundy as they could conveniently manage. The child started and cringed when Lundy snarled at her without warning, but rose at once in response to his summons to secure more food and bring it to him. As he snatched it ungraciously, she slipped back to her mother.

Mavis, after a few tentative words to Eve and the girl, Eva, had returned to the prevailing pattern of watchful silence. But her dark eyes ranged speculatively. Blanchard guessed the turbulence of her thoughts, this fresh wash of uneasiness. For her it was new and strange, increasingly grim. He had been a fool to yield to her insistence, to bring her on such a quest.

Eve was equally silent, but like the others of her group, making sure of a good meal while the opportunity presented itself. For them, like Indians, there would be periods of lean living, interspersed with occasional feasts. Theirs was clearly a nomadic existence.

The men, Lundy in particular, were by nature close enough to the primitive to be at home in such a life, though it probably was not a matter of choice. Like Kearns and his followers, they were outlaws. The difference was mostly in degree.

Silverman, watching with foxlike slyness, seemed content to let events take their course. But Cloud's anger came to the fore.

"I don't like this setup, Jim. This bunch messin' in on our affairs!"

Kearns was caught by surprise. Clearly he wished to avoid controversy, at least for the time being. He wiped his mouth with the back of his hand. Lundy cut in before he could reply.

"Messin' in!" he snarled. "You're the ones that are interferin'. This is our country, back here! You damn well better get rid of any notion that you're going to come here and boss us!"

Kearns answered quickly. He was increasingly uneasy, forced to the conclusion that Blanchard had outthought and outmaneuvered both Lundy and himself.

"None of us had any such a notion," he protested. "But as I've said before, we need to come to some sort of an understanding, to work together. That's the only way to avert disaster. You and I had better talk things over, Tom."

"If Lundy talks, we talk," one of Lundy's companions warned. "We won't stand for no double cross!"

"Close your trap, Swant," Lundy warned. "We'll talk—later, if it's worth takin' the trouble. I ain't so sure it is."

"There's some things that need decidin'," Swant contradicted. His eyes turned to where Mavis sat alongside her father, shadowy in the dying glow from the fire. "You've already got a woman. Gregor and me, we ain't!"

Kearns bristled in sudden outrage. He was clearly having some second thoughts, even regrets for the part he had played in having brought Mavis into this. The complications resulting from this wandering wolf pack had not entered his calculations.

"Let's get a few things straight right now," he snapped. "I've told you before, and that goes for all three of you: These people are our guests! And they're to be treated as such."

Swant shrugged sullenly, but it was Gregor who spoke. His mind was clearly on another possibility, spurred by a thirst not easy to quench in such solitudes.

"You got some whiskey, maybe?" he asked hopefully. "He didn't have none." He gestured disgustedly toward Cooley's motionless figure.

At the mention of liquor, Kearns's eyes took on a momentary gleam. Blanchard could understand. Kearns liked his liquor regularly, and it was a tribute to his determination to keep a clear head on so important an expedition that he had left such supplies behind.

"No, we didn't bring along anything to drink," he returned. "Which is a good thing, all the way around. We need clear heads for finding that strike and handling things—all of us." He jerked his head at Lundy, then moved back into the deeper gloom. After a momentary hesitation, Lundy followed.

Mavis, her face pale in the reflected light, was again trying to get her father to swallow some soup, this time without much success. Cooley remained inert, breathing quietly, but with no signs of returning consciousness. It was an increasingly moot question as to whether that was good or bad.

Blanchard looked around, trying to order his thoughts, to find a way out. Because of their common greed, the truce between the two groups would probably hold for a while, but the prospects were almost as black as the night, which was rendered even blacker by a thickening cloak of clouds. He moved across to Mavis.

She looked around, a questioning uncertainty in her eyes. But her immediate worry was for her father.

"He doesn't respond, or seem to change," she said. "And I—I'm afraid."

"For the present, perhaps it's a good thing that he doesn't change," Blanchard returned, and that needed no elaboration. "We've got to play for time. That's what he needs, as much as the rest of us. If he has it—well, he has great recuperative powers. He told me once that he's as tough as a Texas longhorn, and he sure enough is."

"You've known him well for a long while, haven't you? Whenever he wrote, he was talking about you."

"We've been friends for about half my life, and partners in occasional ventures—like this one. I guess you could say that he's the best friend I've ever had."

"I'm sure he feels the same way about you. Oh, Harry, I'm *so* sorry that I got you into this. I seem to have messed everything up. If it hadn't been for me, having to bother with me, you probably wouldn't have had any trouble."

"Easy now, easy," he protested. "That's just a guess, and he'd have been just the same as he is, only without you to nurse him along. And Kearns would probably have tracked me, and Lundy and his group were in here already. You acted with the best of intentions, and we're in this together. But it could be worse. None of them are our friends, but they hate each other twice as much as they distrust us, and if they find anything, they'll be at each others' throats. Which might work out to our advantage."

"Do you really think so?" She was wracked by a shiver. "They—they are like wolves. Both groups of men. They terrify me. Kearns is smoother, but I'm not certain but what he's the worst of all."

Blanchard could find no rebuttal, for it was an accurate appraisal. He had spoken with more assurance than he felt, but it would be no kindness to hold out false hopes. Both of their lives, as well as Cooley's, were in danger.

Swant had slipped away in the darkness, but Gregor remained, sullenly watchful, as were Cloud and Silverman. It was an armed camp, tense with mistrust, but both groups were united on one point—to keep Cooley, Mavis, and himself under close watch.

Mavis nodded toward Eve and Eva, who were sitting somewhat apart at the opposite side. "I feel sorry for them," she whispered. "Especially the child. What an existence! I take it that you used to know the mother?"

"Eve? Yes, she was right about that. I'd been hurt and was cared for at a mission, and she was there, looked after by the sisters. Not much more than a child herself, at the time. I'm shocked that she'd take up with a man like Lundy."

"It was a mission, you say?"

"A mission to the Indians. I don't remember the name of their order, but those in charge were real sisters of mercy. If it hadn't been for their care, I wouldn't be here now. Eve was shy and lonely. I've often wondered what had become of her, but after I recovered, I never saw her again, or heard of her, until now."

"Poor kid!" Mavis murmured. "Such a life, after a mission! I'm going to talk to her."

She crossed to where the others sat, keeping carefully to the shadows. A low murmur of voices indicated that they were finding some common ground. Blanchard stayed beside Cooley, trying to plan a move, finding none. The lives of all three, Mavis, her father's and his own, could easily hinge on what he did. And a single mistake could be fatal.

Presently Kearns and Lundy returned, moving into the circle of firelight with an appearance of amiability, as though having come to an understanding. Blanchard could guess at its general tenor. Lundy and his crew had come upon Cooley, had probably watched him as he went about his search, perhaps for much of the summer.

By the time he had dispatched the pigeons with their messages, they were sure that he had found what he was after and had tried to force him to disclose his secret. Impatient, their methods had been direct and vicious. Methods that had defeated their own purpose.

Kearns would have pointed out how such bungling had been costly rather than productive. Undoubtedly he had persuaded Lundy that both groups must unite in a common effort to locate the strike, form some sort of partnership. At least, such details could be held in abeyance until there was something to quarrel over.

Having made some common agreement, Kearns was still suspicious, with apparent good reason, Blanchard thought, as he listened to the two men's words.

"But you jumped him, and you say you took him by surprise. *After* he'd made his strike. I know he didn't tell you where it was, but he must have brought back some dust or nuggets, something from what he'd found. It should have been in his camp."

"I reckon he found something, all right, but he sure hid it clever," Lundy returned. "We ain't been able to find even a trace of color. It makes me so mad—"

"Sure, sure, but taking out your mad on him didn't work, and the shape he's in, we've got to help get him well again. Take the best care of him we can manage. There won't be too much time before winter closes in, and if that happens . . ."

"Yeah, that'd spoil it," Lundy agreed. "That's why I tried to make him talk, to hurry things up. I know what this country's like. And talkin' of winter, there's a storm on the way. And when it snows in here, it snows. Those tents—"

He gestured contemptuously to those of Kearns's group, now set up just at the edge of the fireglow, then to Mavis's tent, close by where her father lay. "Get a real storm, they'll come down on top of you, same as a boot on a bug."

Kearns regarded him anxiously. "What's the best thing to do then?" he asked.

"Get ourselves under cover, and them," Lundy returned. "I'll show you. There's a cave, right handy. The old man's been usin' it in bad weather. You got a lantern?"

Kearns produced one from their stock of supplies. Carrying Cooley with strange solicitude, they reached the cave, which was hidden out of sight, but surprisingly near. An overhang of cliff concealed a yawning room, the size of which Blanchard could only guess in the dark. Not that the darkness was complete; it was merely a gloom that obscured details. It was almost the time of full moon, and that made a difference, despite the clouds.

Floor, walls and ceiling were of rock. The roof was fairly high, but not too remote to glimpse in the light of the lantern.

Blanchard set up Mavis's tent again, well sheltered, with Cooley on blankets beside it. As the others made their arrangements, he wrapped up in his own blanket alongside Cooley. For the moment, a truce of sorts prevailed. How long it might last was another matter.

15

A gradual lightening denoted another day, and a look from the cavern mouth showed that Lundy had been an accurate forecaster. Snow was falling, and it had a look more of a winter than a late summer storm. The flakes were not big or wet, but they choked the air, and the ground was white.

Early as it was, the snow would not last long, but with subsequent storms the white stuff would begin to pile. But while this lasted, it afforded a respite. Any search for Cooley's strike would be hampered, if not out of the question, until this fall should melt.

So early a snow was a warning. Time was running out. To be caught, perhaps trapped back in here, would be a risky business under the best of conditions. With circumstances as they were, it could be disastrous.

Blanchard was intrigued by the demonstrated presence of cattle. Some of them were from the original lost herd, others probably their descendants. Somehow they had survived, adapting to their environment much as the longhorns had done to the Texas bush, reverting to a wildness akin to bear or bison. That they were here confirmed Cooley's opinion, the hunch on which he had acted. Blanchard lacked the key, but somehow everything must tie in together.

The others were still asleep. A small rustling sound from the shadowy recesses of the cavern attracted his attention. Standing still, he made out the gleam of a pair of small eyes. Some rodent, probably a mountain rat or perhaps an ordinary pack rat, was ready for winter. They usually made use of the holes and crannies inside caves or in the sheltered recesses of cliffs.

The rat darted away, apparently alarmed at another small sound. Turning, Blanchard sucked in a deep breath. Jeb Cooley had moved. Not only that, but his eyes were open, staring about in bewilderment. As he saw Blanchard, the puzzlement gave way to recognition, a pleased excitement.

"So you got here, Harry! Knew you would, soon as you could manage."

His voice was husky, scarcely above a whisper, but vastly reassuring. Nature, given time, was the great healer. Rest and warmth, after the brutality and neglect, had made a difference, perhaps helped by the few swallows of beef broth Mavis had gotten down him. The coherence of his speech was assurance that he had suffered no lasting ill-effects.

Blanchard was beside him, though with mixed emotions. This was wonderful, but it would present fresh complications, hasten the inevitable showdown. There was no way to hide the change from the others.

"Jeb!" he breathed. "You're better!"

Cooley's grin was undecided. "Guess I must be," he conceded. "Looks like I'm just dreamin' this time, 'stead of wrasslin' with nightmares. That homely mug of your'n looks almost handsome!" His tone changed. "Could you get me a drink? I'm dryer'n a road-runner in a sandstorm."

"I sure will," Blanchard agreed, and turned at another stir. The tentflaps parted and Mavis looked out, clearly aroused by their voices. Flushed and rosy with sleep, she stared wonderingly, then excitement took over at the certainty that her father was awake. She stepped out, fully clothed, her boots in one hand, to drop on her knees beside Cooley.

"Dad!" she breathed. "Oh, Dad—I'm here."

Cooley stared back, his uncertainty revived. He had been hoping that Blanchard would come, but for Mavis to be there was almost past belief.

"Mavis!" he breathed. "It is you, sure enough—or am I still asleep an' dreamin'?"

He had accepted the reality by the time Blanchard returned with water, and he drank thirstily, then seemed improved. Bruises, along with aches and pains, would have healed during his period of unconsciousness. Aside from the lingering effects of illness, a weakness not readily overcome, he was on the road to recovery.

Roused by the talk, the others were taking an interest. They were also pleased and excited at this turn, but their concern sprang from totally different reasons. Kearns hurried up from where he had slept at the mouth of the cave, Lundy only an instant behind. Cooley stared uncertainly, then his face cleared, smoothing with understanding. He needed no blueprint to have the salient points clear.

Kearns greeted him with a booming heartiness.

"Man, Cooley, but it's fine to see you awake and better," he declared. "We've been worried about you, getting back to this country to find you sick and hurt."

"Were you, now?" Cooley returned, with a flash of his usual spirit. "Sure and this dream is fast turnin' back to a nightmare!"

"Everything is only too real, Jeb," Blanchard assured him. "And we're all real enough. Mavis came with me, then these others more or less dropped in on us, as you might say."

"Same as ants at a picnic!" Cooley's whisper held bitter understanding.

With Lundy and his companions staring from the background, Cloud and Silverman at the far side, Kearns was not so crass as to make further protestations of goodwill. No one would be fooled by them, least of all Cooley. Not only had consciousness returned, but his wits as well.

"Sure makes for a surprise party, all you folks," he observed. "'Specially you, Mavis. You came with Harry? You've grown to be like your ma, pretty as a picture. But to persuade him—that must have took some doing."

Mavis understood, and her eyes filled with tears. Blanchard answered.

"And they trailed us in." He gestured toward Kearns.

"And the others I know about," Cooley confirmed. He could not keep the dismay from his tones. "Sort of a mixed blessing. Leaves a man with nothing to say. At least, nothing that's fit to say," he added.

"Don't be bashful on my account, Cooley, but go ahead and say it." Kearns grinned. Cooley's recovery had put him in a high good humor. "But let's stir ourselves. Get a fire going and some breakfast cooking. You must be hungry, Cooley."

"Now that you mention it, I do have an appetite," Cooley admitted. It developed that he had stored a lot of dry wood inside, weeks before. A fire was kindled, and Mavis reheated the broth. But as she prepared to feed her father, Lundy protested.

"Hold up," he ordered. "Strikes me, Kearns, this is a time for doing a little tradin'. Make him talk before he eats."

"Does experience teach you nothing?" Kearns reproved. "Your methods are crude. In any case, we're in no great hurry, the way this storm is coming down."

Lundy gave in with ill grace.

"Sure, it may be gone by tomorrow, but there'll be others. And suppose somebody else shows up—the damn Mounties, for instance?"

Startled, Kearns was instantly wary.

"The Mounties?" he repeated. "You mean the Canadian police? But what'd they be doing here, south of the border?"

"Who knows where the border is, or cares?"

Lundy returned. "Maybe we're some south, but we could as easy be in Canada. Either way, we're close to the line. And they have a way of prowlin'—"

Blanchard listened with sharpened attention. A notion on which Cooley had once speculated recurred to him; that Slade Tatum, turning from other pursuits to driving a herd of cattle, might have been heading not so much for remote and empty country but for the international boundary as well. Why he should want that, Blanchard had never understood, but apparently he had succeeded in reaching such an objective.

"I don't figure we've anything to worry about." Kearns was sarcastic. "Of course, I wouldn't know about you fellows. But we'll handle this my way. You had your chance and bungled it."

Cloud, assisted by Eve and Eva, was cooking breakfast for everyone. The child was quick and eager, and Cloud, to Blanchard's surprise, smiled and did not discourage her efforts.

The uneasy truce held, with mutual distrust but enforced cooperation. How long it would last was a question. Lundy, Gregor, and Swant wolfed their food as before, but Kearns's companions dusted off such manners as they had once known, in deference to the women and child. Eva brought a laden plate to Blanchard, smiling shyly as she presented it.

"I feel like I know you, too," she confided. "Since you and Mommy used to be good friends."

"Thank you, Eva," Blanchard returned. "I'm sure we'll be good friends too."

"I hope so," Eva agreed. "I don't have many friends."

Lundy's snort was eloquent, but he made no comment. Kearns drained a cup of coffee, then went to stare out from the mouth of the cave. Blanchard crossed to stand beside him.

"We aren't friends, Kearns, nor exactly allies, but since we're all mixed up in this together, I'd like to talk to you. Has it ever occurred to you just how heavy the odds are that you're bucking? Leaving out Lundy and his pair of playmates, there are a lot of lives on the board. Which amounts to a lot more than money. They could make for impossible odds."

Kearns nodded, dourly honest. "They're steep, I'll admit. But so are the stakes."

"That applies to all of us. So, under the circumstances, I'm willing to make some concessions, which normally I wouldn't even consider. If you'll work with me to get Jeb Cooley and his daughter safely out of here, out of this mess, then I give you my word that I'll play along with you and make no charges or accusations afterward."

"You mean by that some sort of a partnership when we find the gold?"

"Something of the sort. A reasonable share for everybody should be better than nothing. Mavis being here may change Cooley's mind to some extent—if he's treated reasonably and fair. And we'd be more dependable allies than Lundy and his bunch."

Kearns was obviously tempted, then he shook his head.

"I'm afraid not. Not yet, anyway. If it was you alone, I'd risk it, for your word's good. But there are too many in on this. Sooner or later, after we were out of here, somebody would get drunk and spill the beans."

He scowled at the steadily falling snow, which seemed to be thickening rather than showing signs of lightening for sunrise.

"We all have to stay till this is worked out," he went on. "There's nothing wrong now, since Cooley's doing all right—"

"Nothing wrong, did you say? Unless we get trapped in here by deep snow for the winter?"

"That chance is one more reason for you to persuade Cooley to work with us. Oh, I'm inclined to be reasonable, to go along if it can be managed. And with his girl here, he'll maybe show some sense. . . ."

Meeting Blanchard's faint smile, he colored at the slip of the tongue: he had virtually admitted that it had been his intention from the start to hold Mavis as a hostage.

"Now that he's had his breakfast, he ought to be well enough to talk," Kearns said, and with that he approached Cooley. The others gathered promptly.

"Some things have changed," he observed significantly. "It's to everbody's interest to work together, to develop your strike, Cooley. We can stake and head back as soon as the weather clears, if you'll cooperate."

Cooley looked blank. "How can I cooperate with what I ain't got?" he countered.

"You can cooperate with what you *know,*" Kearns

warned bluntly. "I read the message you sent by one of those pigeons, which made it clear that you've made a real strike. That's how I was able to steal a march on Blanchard. So let's not waste time by playing innocent."

Cooley considered, looking from Mavis to Blanchard and back. Had there been only himself to consider, he, like Blanchard, would have been willing to work with the outlaws. But Mavis's presence made a vital difference.

"Supposing I work along with you? What guarantee do I have that you'll not resort to your usual tricks?"

Kearns's eyes glittered with eagerness. "My word," he returned promptly. "In any case, it's to everyone's interest to work together."

Cooley managed a tired headshake. "Your word ain't worth a cast-off chew of tobacco. But there's one way you can prove good faith. Start Mavis and Harry back, with horses. Once they're far enough along to be safe, and with *everybody else here,* I'll tell you how to find the strike, share and share alike."

Kearns considered, then gave a reluctant consent.

"Fair enough," he agreed. "There should be plenty for everyone—"

"More'n plenty," Cooley assured him.

"Then we'll get right at it—"

"Like hell we will," Lundy cut in heatedly. "That deal may suit you, but it sure as blazes don't go with me! I'll see you all in hell first."

16

Kearns bristled. The struggle for leadership was becoming fiercer, hate as well as greed spurring the rivalry. Surprisingly, he held on to his temper, trying to be reasonable. Elated at Cooley's concession, he saw fortune within his grasp, only to be endangered now by Lundy's refusal to go along.

"What ails you?" he demanded, exasperated. "All the rest of us are trying to make the best of things. It's the only way there is—"

"You're a fool," Lundy cut in harshly. "Ain't you ever seen gold, except maybe after it's minted into money? It don't come that way. It don't even come as nuggets, or dust—not more'n once in a lifetime. You have to dig it out, usually from rock and quartz, which is hard work and takes a lot of time. And how much time'd we have, once those others were out from here and back in town?"

It was a strong argument, though Kearns pointed out its weakness.

"Once we've staked and filed—"

"How—with them ahead of us? And you can't monkey with Canadian law. All we'd get would be the inside of their jails, or worse."

That, Blanchard suspected, was his real reason. He was undoubtedly hiding from the law. Cooley watched and listened but kept his own counsel.

Kearns was won over, at least for the time being. Once the storm ended and the snow melted, a fresh quest by both parties might have better luck. Lundy was hardly appeased.

"Why waste time waiting for what ain't likely to happen?" he demanded. "He knows where he found the stuff, so the thing to do is to make him talk."

"You had a try at that," Kearns reminded.

"Reckon I bungled," Lundy admitted, virtually his first concession. "But things are different now. We've ways of making him tell what he knows—without layin' a finger on him." His glance shifted to Mavis. At the clear implication in words and look, she lost color.

This time, Kearns considered, obviously tempted by the possibilities of such a course, and the true measure of the man was revealed. His headshake was indecisive.

"It hasn't come to anything quite that desperate yet," he temporized. "I still think we'll all do better by cooperation. We have two choices, and that's the best."

Lundy spat his disdain, but did not press the issue. Kearns was weakening, and the course Lundy proposed was tempting, but as a gambler, Kearns kept his eye on the odds. Once embarked on such a course there could be no turning back, no halfway measures. The real difficulty was that there were too many witnesses to whatever atrocities might result.

That was a risk Lundy could afford to dismiss. He was already a wanted man, skulking in such wilderness because he dared not venture close to civilization. But Kearns was anxious to avoid a similar plight. Even if such witnesses could be silenced, other men would pursue an investigation, increasingly curious over Jeb and Mavis Cooley's disappearance, not to mention Blanchard's.

Cooped inside the cavern by the steady fall of snow, tempers showed no improvement as the day wore on. Cloud busied himself with preparing a sizable roast from the butchered steer and turning it on a spindle above a steady blaze. He seemed more than satisfied to keep busy, as though anxious to divorce himself from the quarrel. Gradually, as savory fragrances began to permeate the cave, Lundy turned to assist him with the meal. He searched with increasing impatience among the supplies, then swung with a snarl.

"Who's been stealin' the coffee beans?" he demanded. "I left them right here, and somebody's swiped a bunch since morning." The manifest unlikeliness of such a theft added to his anger. Glaring about, his gaze fixed balefully on Eva as she sat, half-hidden among the shadows, playing solemnly with some toy of her own contriving.

"It's you that's been into it!" he charged. "You're always into something—"

Eva fled as he darted toward her, then stumbled and cried out. Frantically she regained her feet, looking about for refuge. With sure instinct, she darted behind Blanchard.

"Out of my way," Lundy roared, and thrust with splayed fingers against Blanchard's shoulder. "I'll show the brat—"

Blanchard had grown as restless as any, but with the storm confining both groups in so restricted a space, he could find no way to slip out without being seen. He had been on the point, moving slowly, of getting back into the deeper, shadowy recesses of the cavern. Now he was checkmated, but not unwillingly.

"Easy, man," he warned, and Lundy, to his astonishment, was bounced back as though bumping a flexible wall. "You're jumping at a crazy conclusion. Though the poor little kid does look half-starved."

"Are her looks any of your business?" Lundy countered. Here was a vent for his increasing frustration. Jealousy reddened his eyes. "She's a thievin', no-good brat," he added deliberately. "Though maybe that's natural, just like it is for you to stand up for the cub!"

The sly insinuation took Blanchard by surprise. Fear shone large in the child's eyes. Whatever its manifestation, she had long been the butt of his insane jealousy.

The reason for such jealousy was easy to see. Eve had quickly been disillusioned, but circumstances had held her tied to Lundy as the little band wandered in the wilderness. But occasionally her resentment had found expression, especially as Lundy cuffed both mother and child.

As he hurled the accusation, Lundy swung wildly, and Blanchard ducked to the side, then struck out in turn, with all his weight behind the blow. Lundy went down, his nose blossoming like a squashed tomato. Then he bounced upright, bellowing, to fight in the only way he knew, with lashing fists and sudden, treacherous kicks. Blanchard avoided a boot, picked his target, and Lundy sprawled a second time.

This time he did not rebound. His head lifted, swinging sullenly. The child cried a warning.

"He's got his gun!"

One hand, half-hidden as he lay, was starting to lift. Blanchard jumped and kicked. His boot sent the revolver spinning, discharging, the thunder of the explosion muffled yet magnified by the confines of the cavern.

Kearns had watched, startled but alert. He darted now to snatch up the weapon before Blanchard could reach it.

Once again it was an impasse, if not an extension of truce. Lundy got slowly to his feet. He managed an elaborate shrug, nose still bleeding. Clearly he had had enough.

"The damn brat ain't worth fightin' over." He grunted. "Just no good!"

Eva stood, taut and slender. The marks of old whippings showed on her arms and legs. Blanchard was half minded to resume the fight, to chastize the man and perhaps at least teach him circumspection.

But Eve stepped forward, her face white but her eyes scornful.

"He hates her," she explained bitterly. "To him, a woman is just a beast of burden, a convenience, and when slowed or hindered by a baby, that he could barely abide! He is no man, for all his bulk—just a creature who walks on two legs!"

The others had watched tensely. Silverman cackled uncertainly, then swung, his face changing, sniffing. At the same moment, Blanchard became aware of the odor of alcohol. Crossing to the pile of supplies, Silverman looked, then pointed to the shattered fragments of a brown bottle.

"Thought you said you didn't have no whiskey," he said accusingly to Kearns. "But look what he's gone and done, shootin' crazy. The bullet ruined the bottle for fair—and me with tongue hangin' out for a drop of the stuff!"

"All I had was that one bottle, just to be used in case of accident," Kearns protested hastily. "On such a trip as this, I figured it might be needed as medicine. I couldn't treat or divide it. There wouldn't have been more than a swallow apiece."

That was probably true, but the reek of the whiskey was doubly tantalizing now that it was lost. The others had an eager look, but they scowled at Kearns. "I was saving it for Cooley, as a last resort," he added desperately.

Lundy had swung back, eager for a different outlet for his temper. "You're a liar. You was keepin' it for yourself. It's what comes of being willing to fool with outsiders, who are trouble any way you take them."

Beneath so crass a bulk, Lundy possessed a crafty shrewdness. Kearns studied him, realizing his attempt to stir dissension.

"You seem worse scared of outsiders than any of the rest of us," he observed. "Maybe you figure that outside law wouldn't approve of the way you handled Cooley?"

Lundy's face attested to the shrewdness of the guess, then he shrugged.

"To hell with the law," he pronounced. "And with him, too. If I maybe hit him a little harder than I intended, to settle an old score, what's wrong with that? The skunk cheated me, a long time back."

"As usual, you pick on a sick man, who can't defend himself!" Eve was spiteful.

"I say he did me dirt," Lundy insisted. "I'd have been within my rights to kill him!"

17

Cooley's underlying strength and powers of recuperation showed strikingly. He lay quietly, but watchfully, in full possession of his faculties. Given a little time, he would be as good as ever.

"He's lying, as usual," he said quietly, as Kearns's gaze shifted questioningly. "He tried to steal from me, thinking I had something worth the swiping, which wasn't the case, and as usual, he blames everyone but himself for his mistakes."

"It wasn't stealin' to take my share. We was partners, wasn't we?" Lundy demanded heatedly. "Or we was supposed to be."

"I guess we were, supposedly," Cooley acknowledged. "I had been so foolish as to feel sorry for him and take him on. That was back before you'd come to this country, Harry," he added to Blanchard.

"When I found him, he was sick and mighty near starved, and I felt sorry for him. In those days he called himself Metisse, Jean Metisse. I didn't know at the time that the law was after him. The Mounties. I was still pretty much of a tenderfoot myself, in some respects.

"I was even foolish enough, later on, to believe

him when he insisted to me that he was innocent, though he admitted that if he was caught the law would probably hang him. He also gave me a fine story about a wife and small son, how they would starve back in a lonely camp where they were wintering, with no means of getting out unless he returned. I doubt whether he even had a wife in those days, but at the time I believed him."

Everyone was listening with a sharp interest, Blanchard most of all. He had known, indirectly, of some such episode in Cooley's past.

"As I say, I believed him—and mistakenly gave him a chance to escape when the Mounties showed up," Cooley went on tiredly. "After it was too late, I discovered how I'd been rooked. He was guilty of the crime, and if he had a family, they certainly had to shift for themselves. The thanks that I had from him came when we met again, a few days ago. He tried to torture a secret from me, then to kill me."

Given so simply, the story impressed even Lundy's own followers. Instead of looking shamed, it seemed to excite a curious pride in Lundy. To hoodwink others was at least equal to beating them in a physical contest.

"What does any of that matter?" he countered. "He cheated me then, fooling me into thinking that the Mounties were after me, persuading me to run. Later, I found out why. He had already found the gold we were hunting for, and that way he kept it all, my share as well as his. Again now he thinks to cheat me in the same fashion."

The jealous craftiness of the man burst full-throated.

"But this time he made a bad mistake. It would do him no good, not in any case! I can tell what you others are too blind to think about. What if he *has* found a rich strike? It would never do him any good, even if we went away and left him."

Kearns frowned uncertainly. "What the devil are you driving at?" he demanded.

"That other time he cheated me, and now it's catching up with him." Lundy chortled. "I told you before what I thought, and now I know. This is not the States, but Canada! We're north of the border."

Silence fell as those implications were considered. If it were so, a new dimension was added to an already confused situation.

"You sure about that?" Kearns countered.

"Plenty sure," Lundy insisted. "And Cooley's still in bad with the Mounties, from what happened back then. On this side of the border, he can't stake a claim and get away with it."

Kearns lost no time in puncturing that argument.

"Even if you're right, the only difference it'll make is to you. His girl and Blanchard could file, to keep it in the family."

Lundy glowered resentfully. "You *would* have to kick over the beans," he snarled. "You talk to me as to a child, but you're the crazy one."

The snow showed no sign of letting up. The men of both outfits busied themselves with other matters, and for the first time, Blanchard had a chance to talk privately with Cooley.

"I take it that my pigeons made it back?" Cooley asked.

"They sure did," Blanchard acknowledged. "The only trouble was that they fell into Kearns's hands. Mavis arrived at about the same time—and he got to her first."

"No wonder he was able to horn in!" Excited, Cooley raised to an elbow. "It's a sure enough mess."

"I've been thinking of what Lundy said," Blanchard mused. "For your sake, and Mavis's, maybe we should let them have your find. They couldn't start to dig or do any sort of operating before spring, and if they can't any of them file legally . . ." He left the sentence unfinished, knowing that Cooley would understand.

Cooley sank back, his excitement ebbing.

"A lot of things haven't worked quite as I expected," he said. "And as of now, they sure ain't as simple as they sound. I'd sure be tempted, if it would help you and Mavis. But once they found out, we wouldn't have any time! And they wouldn't dare leave any of us alive!" He added a cryptic note. "Slade Tatum had to gamble, too—and he almost made it."

Tatum, and the lost herd! Cooley had no chance to say more, and what he had told seemed to make no sense at all. But Cooley had stumbled onto the secret that had killed Tatum, and it might destroy them all.

18

Mavis reappeared from her tent, her hair combed, outwardly composed and looking as fresh as if she had endured no long and tiring journey, with triple shocks as soon as they had arrived at this valley; to find her father hurt and unconscious, then with the callous coming and intervention of two rival gangs, both unmistakably questing for the treasure.

Blanchard caught his breath at the sight of her. He stared as though he had never seen her before, and certainly he was viewing her with new eyes. Something had been happening to him during those days on the trail, and this was culmination and climax.

She had walked unannounced into his life, and now everything was changed. No longer could he think of her as just another woman, or as Jeb Cooley's little girl. She was that, and more. Such a woman as a man might cherish, even die for.

He checked sharply at that. To die for someone was a romantic ideal, but the thought of dying with or for her was too grim a possibility to be pleasant. More than ever he had to find a way to escape from this, to live along with her.

Color mounted in Mavis's cheeks as her eyes met his, responsive to what she saw in them. Her glance was searching. Understanding her unspoken question, Blanchard could only shake his head. Jeb's helplessness and her own desperate need cried out to him, but at the same time they helped tie his hands.

Had he been alone, he could risk taking chances without too much thought for the consequences. But to blunder now could destroy them along with himself.

There was little chance to talk by themselves, to discuss or plan. The others kept close enough to make sure of that. Lundy had washed away the blood and marks of combat. For the moment, with snow falling steadily, he seemed content to wait.

Blanchard checked a grin as he understood. They were waiting for him, hoping that he would make a move—sure that sooner or later he would have to—and then they would trail him as before, as he led them to the secret they were sure he shared along with Cooley.

They would allow him to slip away, to go where he pleased, up to a point. Well, he would lead them a merry chase. At least it would keep everyone occupied.

To slip away without challenge was easy. Snow fell steadily, so that visibility was reduced to a brief radius. Blanchard moved steadily, employing the full bag of tricks he had learned over a span of years. He wondered who would be the first to realize what he was up to, if any would, or how long it might take. Meanwhile, it was pleasant to turn the tables, even if only on a small scale, to play games with them.

Within half an hour he came upon tracks in the snow, trails beginning to blur with the continued fall, becoming a sort of maze as he kept going and others tried to follow. If they could read such sign they must be angry, uncertain, and disgusted.

If so, they were not the only ones. Blanchard stared about with tightening mouth. Having laid a trail to confuse them, he had struck across to have a look at the horses. Only there were no horses.

Faint traces showed where the animals had been, but the tracks were old, all but smoothed over by new snow. The horses were gone, and that could mean only one thing. One party had worked to outsmart the others, removing the horses to a new meadow, their trail already lost.

Lundy, almost certainly, would have masterminded such a coup. Blanchard doubted that Kearns would have thought of that means for checkmate, or that any of his crew would be capable of carrying it out even if they had had such an inspiration. Only Lundy and his bunch were familiar enough with the country to know of another secure hiding place.

Control of all of the horses gave him an advantage, leaving the rest of them stranded and at his mercy. There was only one real counter in this game for high stakes—the secret of the lost treasure.

Time and the chance for maneuver was running out. And the snow would be letting up within an hour. There should be enough cover for what he really had in mind—exploration not out here but inside the cave. Hopefully, most of both crews would be wandering outside, trying to watch each other and himself.

A lot of imponderables remained, but some pieces, incomprehensible until now, were falling into place. Factors such as Cooley's attitude, along with the ambiguous remarks he had made at the outset.

Luck was with him. Watching for his chance, Blanchard slipped back inside the cave when no one was around to notice, then lost himself in the gloomier recesses. The reflection from the snow supplied a measure of light.

Briefly he pondered what to do with the supply of whiskey he had brought. Such liquor was a worry, and might be dangerous, but for the present at least it was too perilous to try and retrieve it.

Somewhere in the gloom he caught a small rustling sound. A gleam of eyes shone redly, and he saw the outlines of a small rat. Such small dwellers of the mountains had a liking for the shelter of caves.

Squatting down, he spoke softly, holding out a hand.

"Nothing to worry about, old fellow. I'm wondering if you and Jeb made each other's acquaintance during the summer—maybe got to be friends? Jeb likes all sorts of birds and animals, and I expect both of you found it lonesome at times, eh?"

The rat came erect on its hind feet, clearly not alarmed. It seemed likely that this part of his hunch was also correct.

"You like animals too, don't you?"

The soft voice startled him, but Blanchard only turned his head, then answered the child's smile, which he sensed rather than saw. Eva extended her hand to the rat, a few crumbs of food on her palm. The rat hesitated, then approached and took the offering.

"So that's where the coffee beans went," Blanchard reflected. "And you've been risking Lundy's bad temper to swipe stuff to feed your pet?"

"I took only a little, and he was hungry," Eva explained. "Besides," she added matter-of-factly, "Lundy had stolen it to begin with."

"And you've tamed the rat. You've been here at the cave before, I take it?"

"We camped just outside for a while last spring," Eva explained. "Before *he* came to set up *his* camp. I could not quite get the rat to come and eat, then. This time, it is much tamer."

Apparently Lundy wandered rather widely through the back country, hunting and fishing, perhaps prospecting occasionally.

"And then you folks came back a few days ago?"

"Yes. That was when we showed ourselves, and Lundy tried to make your friend tell him where his gold was. Mama tried to stop Lundy, but she could not."

"And I suppose that for the most part you folks just wander around?"

"We have to," she explained. "We've nowhere to go. Besides, he would kill us if we tried to get away. He's so afraid that the law will find him again."

"We'll find a way to change that, before we're done," Blanchard promised. "You and your mother deserve a chance at a decent life."

"Mama said that you would find some way," Eva agreed confidently. She smiled, then was gone as silently as she had come. The rat had vanished also.

The extent of the cavern was surprising. It was huge. He felt his way in the gloom, then paused, aware that he was climbing over a pile of rough and broken rock and debris. A slip in the dark could be dangerous.

Again there was a rustling sound, then he made out the rat, or another. Almost absently at supper he had slipped a chuck of biscuit into a pocket, with something of the sort in mind. He held it out, wondering if this rat would accept food from him.

It advanced in a quick scurry, then sat erect, whiskers twitching, eyes watchful. Dropping back to all fours, it came on, halting at intervals. Blanchard addressed it softly.

"It's all right, old fellow. Your friends are mine. And if you're hungry, why—come and get it!"

Cocking its head, the rat appeared to consider, then retreated as angry voices sounded from the camp. When they subsided, it came back, cradling a small object between its paws. Placing the object almost at his feet, it scampered away, then stopped to watch.

That was a characteristic of trader rats, or pack rats, as they were known. Blanchard took it up in polite acceptance, then looked closer with a suddenly hammering pulse. What it had fetched was no ordinary pebble. He hardly needed a closer scrutiny to be certain that its gift was a gold nugget, much larger than the average.

But if this was a clue to Cooley's strike, he was more than ever bewildered and confused. All his calculations were in danger of being upset.

19

A closer examination, despite the dim light, convinced him that it was indeed gold. But in place of elation, he was bewildered.

The rodent's part was understandable. Inquisitive by nature, it had probably investigated Jeb Cooley's supplies, helping itself whenever it discovered any small article that took its fancy. In exchange, again in accordance with its nature, it would present the man with a pebble or some small token. Jeb, spending the summer amid vast and almost awesome silences, would have welcomed such companionship, making the rat something of a pet.

But a nugget . . .

Apparently there *was* gold hereabouts, though in what amounts Blanchard had no idea. And whether Cooley had made a discovery or not he could only guess. A notion was forming in his mind, a plan in which the nugget might be useful. Gold was what both parties of outlaws sought, treasure for which they would stop at nothing to obtain.

The rat, as well as its gift, increased the chances of what he had already suspected—another entrance or exit from the cavern. Apparently that possibility had not occurred to Lundy; otherwise he would have pursued his search within the cavern. Or it could be that he had been deterred by a superstitious awe of such cavernous and shadowed depths.

Wizards and necromancers had sought an alchemy in gold, and however different in degree, it was unlocking possibilities in his mind, suddenly jumping with ideas. If there was a back door, another way out . . .

Moving carefully, the squeak of another rat drew his glance to the side, and for an instant fiery eyes glared back, then vanished. His searching look discovered a small opening in what had seemed to be solid wall. Abruptly he was between impulses, as a gleam, faint but unmistakable, loomed high and distant beyond. That could only be daylight.

Puzzled, he finally understood. Somewhere between himself and the light a shoulder of rock or outthrust had cut off all view of it, but from this angle it was visible, a secret that could easily go unnoticed even in a determined search.

By comparison with what the light meant the small opening was secondary, but it would take only a minute to look it over. On hands and knees he entered. The doorway was big enough but with little to spare. A musty smell pervaded the place.

Almost at once the opening enlarged to a room of considerable size, but how big he could only guess in the total darkness. He fumbled for a match, though so feeble a light would be all but lost in such immensity. Still, it might give an idea of the place.

He scratched it, then recoiled at the light and what it revealed almost immediately in front of him. Even an eager hunter, if any had penetrated this far, might have been turned back by the grim specter who poised like a guardian of the cavern—a figure perhaps standing sentinel over hidden treasure such as Jeb Cooley had come seeking.

A tattered shirt still clung, covering skeleton arms. One of the bony fingers still clutched in a death grip a rusting gun; the glow of the match reflected on the steel barrel. Blanchard had no time to see more, as the match went out.

The covering darkness was scarcely a relief, knowing what it hid. Blanchard found himself shaking, as much from surprise as shock. Then the initial effect passed. It was understandable, with what he had discovered or guessed, even logical. Still, the discovery of a man long dead was neither pleasant nor of a sort to soothe the nerves.

But this, almost certainly, explained a considerable part of the riddle, the long mystery connected with Slade Tatum and the herd of cattle he had so inexplicably driven to this remote wilderness near the border. Whether the man with his gun still held in readiness to guard treasure, which must be somewhere farther in the recesses of this room off the big cave, was Tatum or someone else did not particularly matter. Since he had contrived to move the treasure this far, out from under the noses of others who had known that he had it and who had been determined to steal it from him, it must be there.

Tatum and his crew, the latter gradually coming to understand the magnitude of the sum involved, might have quarreled among themselves. Or perhaps the others, whom he had feared and gone to such lengths to deceive, had finally caught up and attacked. In any case, this was the end of the trail.

Blanchard had no doubt that Cooley had found the hiding place, perhaps aided like himself by the pack rats. His message by pigeon confirmed that he had been successful in his quest. And he had cannily protected his discovery.

Confronted, perhaps murdered in a final shootout, Tatum had defended his treasure, then maintained grim guard across the years. Propped against a shelf of rock and held in place by it as he died, the specter of so grim a gunman would send most looters to panic-stricken flight.

Blanchard's breathing eased to normal as he considered. Anxious as he was for a better look, that would require a lantern or a good torch. In any case, further search must be postponed. It would be safer to keep away than to risk the disclosure of so vital a secret.

Backing out of the room, he worked his way toward that distant gleam of light, barely visible. It was farther than it had appeared to be. He climbed gradually, forced to move cautiously in the all but total gloom, ascending as the cavern floor trended upward. This hollow in the mountain was immense, vastly bigger than it had appeared from the camp near the mouth.

But the growing light assured an exit, though

whether it would be usable or not he was far from sure. It was a small crack in the roof of the cavern, the light revealing a mountain of rubble below. At some long distant time a heavy strain or pressure must have caused the break, sending tons of debris to form the mound.

That was handy in turn, providing a platform on which to climb to the break. Reaching it, there was room to squeeze through the crack, though with even a few pounds' greater girth he could never have made it.

It was only a crust of roof, and his head emerged into the outer night, luminous with the effect of the declining moon, on a wide blanket of snow. There had been more snow while he was in the cavern, followed by a clearing.

He had been longer than he had realized, for breaks in the clouds showed that night was close. Everyone, Kearns and Lundy in particular, would be wondering where he had gotten to, increasingly suspicious and apt to be bad-tempered. He should be getting back. But having found this much, he had to know more. The nucleus of a plan was beginning to shape itself in his mind.

He had found another exit, a back door to the cavern, and while there was a better than average chance that Jeb Cooley had discovered it, Blanchard doubted that Lundy or the others had any suspicion of such a way in or out.

High as it was, due to the rising slope of the cave floor and its place in the ceiling, he blinked, somewhat astonished, at what was revealed. The hill of the cavern was overreached by a faintly luminous mass that stood even higher. At first glance it seemed only the edge of another hill, shrouded by snow. Then he sucked an understanding breath, equally compounded of astonishment. The vast mass that stretched away was a hill of ice.

Glacier! There could be no doubt, as he studied it. Any of the recent snowfalls would soon melt, but age-old ice was another matter, and this was glacier country. Hidden behind the hills, this mass had made a slow creep of centuries, grinding to a halt in a cul-de-sac where the mountains pinched together in a V. At one time, decades or centuries before, the sprawl of relentlessly moving ice had perhaps overtopped the cavern itself.

But time brought change, in this case a slow warming that was melting the exposed foot of the glacier, causing a gradual retreat. Not one to be measured in miles or even rods—more likely in feet or inches; a change all but imperceptible until viewed after a shift of years.

That change was apparent from where Blanchard looked down. The bulk of the glacier was perhaps a score of feet beyond, a pronglike mass outthrust and towering above, tons of frozen snow and water that looked so precariously balanced that it might topple at any moment.

Since it had probably looked that way for months or years, the imminent risk was not great. Below, except for the fresh covering of the latest snow, was an open space, some twenty feet across by twice that width. A space cleared by the slow melt, after being covered for centuries by more than a hundred feet of ice.

Studying the V, the trap into which the force of gravity had forced the ice, Blanchard could hazard a guess as to where that nugget the rat had presented to him had come from—a chunk of gold, among other debris pushed and shoved from higher in the hills by the relentless movement of the glacier. A nugget was finally revealed to an exploring rodent when the warming trend had set the glacier back from advance to a slow retreat.

And if there was one nugget, there might be others—perhaps littering the ground below to a depth of inches or even feet! He wondered if the discovery had been as much of a surprise to Cooley as it was to himself.

20

Blanchard could think of no more ironic situation. If his guesses were correct—and the evidence supported them—there was more treasure back in here than anyone had supposed, wealth far in excess of the needs of all of them. Logic would point to a partnership, a division along amicable lines.

But gold fever did not run its course like ordinary distempers of the system, followed by a normal recovery. As had been the case with Jeb Cooley and Tom Lundy years before, the excess of a discovery multiplied hate and greed. A man might share his last crust, but he would snarl like a wolf if a bonanza was the stake.

Blanchard squirmed back through the crack in the roof of the cavern, then made his way past the side room with its endlessly waiting guardian. He had a strong hunch as to what Tatum and his crew quarreled over, but there was no time to confirm it.

Dusk seemed to penetrate more strongly through the mouth of the cavern, and a glimpse of sky beyond told him of a change in the weather. The storm had ended. With sunshine and warmth, the ground covering would soon melt. It was a shift that, if he worked matters right, might be turned to account.

The others, clustered near the entrance, were in a state of excitement. Silverman, still wearing a heavy coat, had clearly just returned from exploring on his own, and was the center of interest. Blanchard held back.

"Gone?" Kearns's voice was a blend of dismay and disbelief. "But I don't understand. They can't be . . ."

"Just the same, they are," Silverman insisted. "Somebody's got away with the horses—aimin' to set the rest of us afoot, I reckon, and have us at his mercy."

His conclusion tallied with the one at which Blanchard had already arrived, but it precipitated a shouting match, questions and accusations, both groups regarding the other with undisguised suspicion. The anger on both sides seemed genuine, spurred by apprehension. Lundy glared angrily.

"Where's Blanchard?" he demanded. "You were supposed to keep an eye on him—"

"I'm here," Blanchard reminded quietly, stepping forward. "What's all the excitement about?"

Lundy's reply was a counterquestion. "Where've you been?"

"Back in there. Looking around, as well as I could. It's too dark to see much."

"You find anything?"

"Hard to tell. Something that might be worth

investigating, if we had plenty of time. But what's this other, that Silverman was so excited about?"

Charges and counteraccusations were angrily exchanged. The loss of the horses could be vital, affecting everyone, but Blanchard, still watching from the sidelines, could not decide who was responsible. He was startled, catching Jeb Cooley's glance, to see one of Cooley's eyes close in an amused wink.

Since Cooley could not have been the rustler, he was telling Blanchard something—obviously, not to worry unduly. After a summer of exploration, Cooley would know this country at least as well as Lundy and his group.

Whoever had moved the horses would have had an adequate hiding place in mind, which narrowed it to Lundy or one of his men. Jeb was obviously trying to tell him that he had found such a place and knew the secret. On that point there was no need to worry.

But the others were worried, almost to the point of desperation, Lundy no less so than Kearns. Was one of his own group pulling a fast one on him? If so, that opened up a whole new field of possibilities.

Kearns again demonstrated why he was a leader, cutting through the confusion of argument and recrimination.

"We're wasting time," he pointed out. "Whether the horses have only gotten loose or been stolen, there's snow for tracking, but it won't last long. What are we waiting for?"

Lundy scowled, then gave grudging approval.

"Sometimes you make sense," he admitted. "Let's have a look. And I mean every man, except for Cooley."

Under less stringent conditions, Blanchard would have been amused. Lundy and his henchmen were enough at home in such country to survive, but neither they nor Kearns's group could be rated as woodsmen. Or perhaps a certain amount of blundering was deliberate, to obliterate and confuse such sign as remained by adding fresh trails, while the deepening dusk seemed to share eagerly in the game.

The chill, induced by storm, had given way to a warming, almost a return of summer. By morning, at this rate, the fresh fall of snow would be only a memory.

The sharp crack of a rifle, from fairly close at hand, brought Blanchard about in a quick turn. There was nothing to see, aside from Lundy and Kearns, who were both in view and were as obviously keeping each other in their own range of vision. They were eyeing each other suspiciously, and with surprise.

A sudden high scream, a blend of pain and terror, sent them all on a run toward the sound. It ended almost as abruptly as it had begun, broken off or smothered in the middle of a high note. That, obviously, was not some sort of acting, but starkly genuine.

Blanchard topped a slope, breaking through a screen of trees, and the other searchers, attracted by the same sounds, were converging as well. Ahead was an open meadow, a couple of acres in extent. At the far side a confused mass sprawled, darkly red against the snow. Sounds had ended, and for the moment there was no movement, no indication of struggle.

Blanchard was ahead of the others, with only a partial understanding. The rifle shot had obviously been for one of the big steers, a giant specimen whose brand showed clearly that it was another survivor of the original lost herd. The sound of the gun, followed so quickly by the scream of the hunter, indicated that the bullet had been discharged at almost point-blank range, and the signs of what had followed were clear enough.

Beyond much doubt the heavy lead had knocked the steer down, and the hunter had rushed at it, substituting a heavy-bladed knife for the rifle. Steer and man lay sprawled together, the man caught, impaled on the sweep of horns, knife still clutched in one hand. Gregor.

Lundy was swearing, twisted between shock and incomprehension. The tableau was exposed for everyone to see, but on its surface it was incredible, beyond understanding. That Gregor should shoot the big steer upon sight, with an eye to securing more meat, was easy to explain. But it seemed the act of a madman or fool to rush upon it with a butchering knife, to be in such mad haste to stick and bleed it when there was no need for hurrying and with the ever-present possibility that an animal, though down, might revive in a final desperate struggle.

That, all too clearly, had happened. One horn had entered Gregor's chest. It protruded through his back.

Both animal and man were dead. The others, of both groups, stared in disbelief. Gregor should certainly have known better. Neither sympathy nor regret was reflected on any face, only shock. Gregor was not a man to be missed.

"The crazy fool!" Lundy said, still with disbelief. "Whatever made him lose his head that way?"

Blanchard was reasonably sure that he could answer that question, though he was startled that the always stolid, stupid-seeming Gregor should have independently arrived at a conclusion so close to his own. A theory which, in his eagerness to confirm, had led him to commit the cardinal sin of the hunter.

21

Lundy and Swant pulled their companion loose, blood spurting as they did so. Lundy obviously was more concerned with the new implications than with the tragedy that had overtaken his henchman. Now he had only Swant to side him. There was Eve, but not only was she a woman but her loyalty to himself and his cause was open to doubt.

Outwardly he gave no sign of such speculation. His shrug was acceptance.

"Too bad, but it can't be helped. Go get a shovel, Joe, and we'll bury him. The rest of you better skin the critter and butcher it. The hide might come in handy, and he was after the meat."

As he had expected, the brunt of that task fell to

Blanchard, though under the circumstances he was not adverse. He took the big knife that had led to Gregor's downfall, then set to work. Skinning or cutting up a big animal was not nearly as easy as it looked at the hands of an expert. Silverman, working to assist but without much enthusiasm, cut his own thumb and swore.

"Better get an axe and chop it up," he growled. "That critter's as old as time, and twice as tough."

He looked for permission to go for an axe, but Blanchard shook his head.

"And ruin the skin?" he countered. "You heard what Lundy said. He's right about that; the hide may come in handy. No telling how long we may be back in here."

Kearns had been shocked to silence. They assisted, but were not very helpful. To peel the hide from a winter-coated steer, as old and tough as this survivor of Slade Tatum's original herd, was anything but easy. They drew back as their knives dulled, more than willing to leave the difficult part to Blanchard. He worked grimly, bending over the still-warm carcass, excitement a stimulant. He no longer particularly needed confirmation for his hunch, but it might be at hand.

The point of the knife encountered something, tougher even than the hide itself, an object at once solid but alien. Fingering through the heavy coating of concealing hair, he knew a wild surmise. With the brand as testimony that this animal had belonged to the original herd, he could hazard a not-too-wild guess.

Holding his face expressionless, he made a deeper incision with the knife, cutting through the steer's heavy dewlap. That was a meaningful location, the obstruction long hidden in the fleshy sag of the skin.

Slade Tatum had been the first to see and appreciate the possibilities, but it had remained for Jeb Cooley to figure out what must have happened, to come on the trail of Tatum's herd.

The others were drawing back, slicing steaks from the skinned-out rump, taking them to the camp for supper. It was that time of day, and that chore provided a good excuse for leaving the remainder of the skinning to Blanchard. He made no protest, instead exploring with his fingers the object that, long buried in the fleshy folds of the dewlap, had turned the point of the knife.

It was roughly shaped, as large as a good-sized marble. Risking no more than a quick glance, he concealed it in the palm of his hand, then casually transferred it to a pocket.

Tatum had been a man of mystery from his first appearance in the country, an object of curiosity mixed with suspicion. Blanchard recalled what he had heard of his activities—the rumors of ill-gotten wealth, Slade's purchase of a herd of cattle and departure with them not toward a market or even another ranch but north by west, into ever deeper wilderness. Clearly the behavior of a man touched in the mind—or with some dark secret.

His activities had come to a tragic and untimely end in the recesses of the cavern.

Jeb Cooley had hardly been guessing. He had

followed a hunch, figuring things out to a logical conclusion. It had been a case of fitting forgotten facts together.

The survivors of the lost herd had told him where to search. To discover the treasure had been less easy. He might well have stumbled upon it through the agency of the pack rats, those busy but methodical little animals who helped themselves when some trinket appealed to them, then, with a strange code for trading, replaced it with something else—a pebble, a stick of wood, or—as had been tendered to himself—a gold nugget.

With the trophy from the ancient steer in his pocket, the missing links in the chain of evidence were almost complete. He now knew the secret that had almost cost Cooley his life, that had caused Gregor's careless haste, and, unless he played his cards well, could still charge them all dearly.

Everyone but Mavis appeared to enjoy the steaks, however tough and stringy. Even Jeb masticated a slice with improving appetite, but Mavis was too shocked by the turn of events to eat much. Gregor had been an enemy and dangerous, but he had been one of a suddenly shrinking company, and the implications were not pleasant.

Reaction, with such a man as Lundy, was predictable. More than ever he must assert himself, dominate the others and circumstance as well. A big fire, at the cave entrance, dispelled only a few shadows in its recesses, but after eating he turned to stare speculatively at Blanchard, recalling what he had said of having looked around. Clearly he was arriving at the conviction that the treasure was concealed somewhere in or about the place.

Helping himself to one of the lanterns Kearns had brought along, he prowled uneasily, driven by greed and curiosity, but hesitant to go far. Blanchard was forced to wait with the others, none of them anxious to precipitate a crisis. The opportunity for which he had hoped, to give him a chance to make his own play, now seemed farther away than ever.

An exultant whoop startled them. Casting shadows that loomed gigantic, Lundy came toward the fire, the lantern swinging, clutching something in his other hand. His face showed triumph, a wild elation. Blanchard's heart sank. This was the last straw. Prowling in the dark, Lundy had stumbled upon his hiding place, and he brandished the whiskey bottles for everyone to see.

"So you lied to me, Kearns," he chortled. "Said you didn't have no whiskey. What's this stuff supposed to be—water? Or mebby firewater."

Kearns's surprise and bewilderment were so genuine as to be convincing.

"Those aren't ours," he protested. "Must belong to Cooley—or Blanchard."

"Yeah? Well, it don't matter now." A crafty mask of false gravity spread over Lundy's face. "Sure tough, the way poor old Gregor had to go. I reckon the least we can do is drink a sort of remembrance to him. Which we'll do—within limits."

With powerful teeth he wrenched the cork from a flask, tipped it, and drank deeply, not even choking on the fiery potion. His eyes had a new glitter as he lowered the bottle and tendered it to Kearns.

"Since we're partners, more or less, you and your friends can drink too. But jus' you folks 'n us. Not the rest. They ain't for us—and whiskey ain't good for them, anyhow."

The flask went the rounds, with Blanchard and Cooley, the women and child forced to watch uneasily. By the time the no-longer rival gangs had sampled it, one flask was empty.

Lundy eyed the remaining bottle speculatively, with the possible thought for reserving it for some future occasion. But the taste for liquor, long unfilled, drove them now. He twisted the second cork loose.

Blanchard made his move. It was now or never. With the second bottle they would be roaring drunk, beyond inhibitions. Torture and worse . . . poor as was the moment, he had to take the chance.

The small sound of an object striking the rocky floor drew all eyes. Lundy gaped as he focused on the dull glitter of the nugget and lowered the untasted flask.

22

Reality frequently falls short of expectation, and that was the case now. They had dreamed so long of gold, seeking it so determinedly, that the nugget, with all that it implied, left them bemused and uncertain.

Lundy glared about. He had undergone a change, since the revelation that he was Jean Metisse, a metamorphosis like grub into moth, though about him there was nothing of the butterfly. He was the leader now, Kearns subjected to a secondary role and, not too strangely, accepting it.

"Where'd this come from?" Lundy snatched it up, holding it to the light, juggling it on his palm for weight. His voice was hoarse. "One of you—" His glance focused, almost accusingly, on Blanchard.

Blanchard nodded. "Sure," he agreed. "I wanted to get your attention—before it was too late."

He had it, beyond any doubt. At a loss, Lundy took recourse in bluster.

"What do you mean, too late? You beginnin' to

understand that I'm runnin' things here?"

"If you are, you're doing a damn poor job," Blanchard returned bluntly. "You'd all be drunk in a little while, then ugly, after which you'd have to sleep it off. That way, even if nothing worse happened, a couple of days would be lost, and by then there'll be another storm hitting in here. Once a real storm does come, the gold will be out of sight and out of reach for at least half a year."

Scowling, Lundy thought that over, as suspicious as a wolf of a trap. But the nugget was convincing.

"I'd think that'd suit you fine," he pointed out.

"It would, ordinarily," Blanchard admitted. "But not at the price of having you crazy drunk, then being trapped in here with no way of getting out. I prefer a trade, to show you the gold, for our lives. And I can do it now, all because a pack rat brought me that nugget and showed me where to look."

The silence was heavy, broken only by the snap of a stick of firewood, the flame flaring higher, then falling away. The nugget was proof that Blanchard knew what he was talking about, and it gave him leverage for bargaining. His offer to reveal the secret of the strike carried weight.

"You mean, it's back in here?" Lundy was incredulous, even as he gestured to encompass the cavern.

"It's not," Blanchard denied flatly, aware of the surprise in Jeb Cooley's eyes, and bewilderment in the faces of the others. "But it's close. And while I haven't had a chance to really test it, I've an idea that it's tremendously rich—and in loose dirt and gravel, dust and nuggets, not ore that would have to be mined and hauled and smelted."

That half-promise whet their appetite as the sight of the flasks had done. Raw gold in the shape of nuggets would be a bonanza that they could handle, spendable wealth. The other, no matter how rich, would be hopelessly beyond their reach.

Lundy wet his lips. "What you got in mind?"

"Save that liquor to celebrate with, after you have the gold. Put it away for now and get some sleep. The gold's not easy to get to or at. We'll have to have daylight. I'll show you tomorrow."

They were still uncertain, like hounds on leashes, but his flat promise impressed them. The assurance that the strike was not inside the cavern bolstered their lack of discovery after a desperate search.

He was offering them a choice along with a promise, and there was no real alternative. Reluctantly, Lundy stalked into the gloom, then returned without the bottle. For a few minutes he discussed these newest developments, talking excitedly with Kearns and his crew. There was an air of amiable cooperation, which did not fool Blanchard. Strong liquor could drive men wild, but it was as nothing to the effect of gold, nuggets that could be juggled and clutched.

Watchfulness on the part of their captors was relaxed. His story that a pack rat had furnished him the necessary clue, rather than a word from Cooley, they accepted at face value. None would have believed another, but they took Blanchard's word.

Blanchard moved into the shadows, and Mavis was at his side. Her voice was subdued, but tense with the common excitement.

"You're really gambling, aren't you, Harry? But didn't you owe it to—to Dad, to get his permission?"

"I would have, if it had been his strike," Blanchard agreed, and his words left her staring in perplexity. "I've a lot to do. I want to talk to him. Warn me if anyone tries to slip up on us."

He reached Cooley's side, the surprise in his partner's face replaced by approval. A prospector was inherently a gambler, and this was a chance-taking after Jeb's own heart.

"Go to it," Jeb urged. "I don't know just what you've got in mind, but I'm betting my shirt you'll pull it off."

"We're betting more than our shirts." Blanchard nodded. "Do you have any dynamite left?"

Jeb wasted no time with questions.

"A couple of sticks."

"Are you strong enough to get them before morning—have them fixed with fuses and caps, both separate? I'm going to be busy with other things."

"They'll be ready," Cooley promised quietly.

Blanchard drew a long sigh of relief. That had been a part of the gamble, that Jeb would have at least a few sticks of explosive left, cached somewhere within reach. If not, there would have been no choice but to turn to Kearns, who undoubtedly had included some among his supplies. Kearns and Lundy would furnish him with what he asked, but to make effective use of it if they had forewarning would complicate an already difficult task.

The others were accepting the situation, not only because there was no choice but because of their relaxed mood as the whiskey took effect. Initially a stimulant, the drink soothed in turn. Well fed and tired, they were in a mood to get a good sleep, in anticipation of the next day's hunt.

Blanchard lay down in his accustomed place, but within minutes only a rolled-up blanket remained. Then he was outside, a night star-hung and luminous with the snow that still remained. But the warm air held above freezing, the melt continuing. Morning should show bare ground.

At this time of year, such clement weather was likely to be followed by storm—a heavier fall of snow that was more likely to last, storm piling on storm. From their own knowledge, Lundy and the others had recognized Blanchard's warning as the truth.

There was a lot to be done, a job that would require a lot of luck, but if his hunch was correct, the horses were not far from where they had originally been held. It would have been impossible to move them very far, as well as undesirable. When needed, they must be within easy reach.

Fortunately, the nights were long. If he was lucky . . .

He had better be, here as later. Each step now depended on the others, all in unison. One misstep could ruin everything. But without the horses, on hand when needed, none of the rest would count.

He had made a quarter of a mile, moving briskly, when a sound caused him to spin about, suddenly tense. Trouble had a way of coming when least expected. He would have been prepared for it from Lundy or Kearns, but not at all from Joe Swant. But it was Swant who eyed him with an uncertain grin.

23

Swant broke the silence. He made no move for his gun, and his voice was mild, though edged with excitement.

"You want the horses, I reckon? I'll show you." He was clearly uneasy, faintly apologetic.

"Maybe you could find them, but likely not. It's kind of a tricky place, unless you know it. I was lucky here a few weeks ago. Saw a cow just sort of disappear, and that got me curious. I followed, and it was a mighty good hiding place. So I moved the horses there during the day."

"And Lundy doesn't know?"

"He takes me for a fool. This time, he's the one that's fooled. Was that right, what you said about the gold?"

"As right as I can figure it, without a chance to dig and make a test."

"That's good enough for me—Eve says you're a straight shooter." His voice was suddenly hoarse with passion. "I can take a lot of kickin' around for myself, but Lundy ain't going to kick her around—not any longer! With you here, and maybe enough gold so we wouldn't starve, that gives us a chance to make a break, to start fresh. I aim to see that Eve and Eva get their chance. And that you'll give us one, for helping."

Blanchard was not much surprised. Lundy's little band had submitted with a quiet resignation, but a mounting desperation. Their arrival on the scene, coupled with the sudden demise of Gregor, had altered everything. Gregor would stand with Lundy, no matter what. Now the odds had shifted.

"You and Eve like each other?"

"She deserves a lot better'n she's had. I ain't much, but we like each other. Reckon I'll have to kill him—but that'll be a pleasure." His tone was grim.

Blanchard eyed him speculatively.

"With your gun, and going back to take them by surprise—that could save a lot of chance-taking in the morning."

"Reckon we'd better take the chances according to whatever you had in mind," Swant returned. "Sure, I've got the gun, but no shells. Lundy's seen to that, ever since you folks showed up. He don't trust nobody but himself."

That altered the situation, as well as explaining Swant's behavior. Swant had played it cagily, but even a rabbit could be pushed beyond the point of desperation.

The terrain was more broken, trees and brush adding to the look of wilderness. A few faint tracks remained in the sinking snow, some belonging to native dwellers such as fisher or rabbit, coyote or bobcat. Others had the look of cattle, then Blanchard made out horse sign.

This had seemed an unlikely territory in which to look for the lost cayuses. Without Swant he might easily have searched in vain.

A trail of sorts had been beaten in what little snow had reached the ground past the shelter of leafy branches. Such trails in wild country would go unnoticed.

The way led along a narrowing route, hemmed by trees and cliffs, trending abruptly downward, a steep trail gradually enclosed by the hills. It was a reasonably easy trail that curved and dropped, never very wide, but not uncomfortably narrow or risky.

"This is sure a funny place," Swant said. "I had a look after that critter showed me the way. The trail runs maybe two or three miles like this. Ends up in a big valley. Hills all around, and as near as I could make out, this is the only way in or out. Lots of good grass down there, and water.

"It gave me an idea. That big cave wouldn't be a bad place to spend the winter for folks that wander the way we've been doing, with Lundy leadin' us. But I got to thinkin' that down in here it could be quite a bit warmer than the rest of the country, being lower the way it is and everything. A right nice place to winter. But I kept it to myself."

Blanchard listened with sudden understanding. He had puzzled over the survival, across a span of years, of Slade Tatum's lost herd. Half-wild cattle could quickly revert to a totally primitive existence, as the

Texas longhorns who had managed to subsist for generations in the bush had demonstrated. There they had fought off predators, adapted to the sometimes scanty and often strange diet, and increased enormously.

But the bush country of Texas was vastly different from so northern a clime as this. Horses could paw away snow and reach grass, surviving under rigorous conditions. Cattle were not usually so adaptable. Still, a number of the original herd, and probably many of their descendants, had managed to live.

This valley was undoubtedly the answer. Instinct or chance had led them to the entrance of the trail that led to this lower, warmer valley. There was probably a lot less snow, making easier living conditions through the winters. Enough easier, at least, that they had adapted and done very nicely.

Again, the instinct of wild creatures had warned them that the hidden valley could quickly be overgrazed, becoming a trap instead of haven. Responding like migrating birds or animals, they moved up and out at the approach of summer, returning when winter threatened. That might account for the number of animals they had seen in the last few days. As wary and hard to spot as deer or elk during the summer, they were increasingly visible as they moved back to their wintering valley.

Swant checked in sudden dismay.

"They've busted out," he exclaimed. "Now we're in trouble. I didn't think they could manage," he added miserably. "But look at that! I found dead trees right off in that little meadow and put up poles to make a gate after I had the horses beyond this point."

The tumbled poles lay on the ground, a maze of fresh tracks in the soft earth. Swant was stricken.

"They must have got nervous, after running and exploring the valley and figuring it was just a big corral, a sort of trap. I sure never figured on that. But they've come back up the trail, making a headlong rush, and smashed right through. By now, they'll be halfway back to town."

His face showed haggard under the light of high stars.

"With more snow in this country, and everybody afoot—it'd be touch and go at best. And with Lundy crazy for gold..."

It could be a serious, perhaps a fatal setback, but Blanchard was looking more closely at the tumbled poles. None of them had been broken, and his respect grew for this supposedly dumb backwoodsman. He was not at all the bungler that he accounted himself.

The poles, obviously, had been placed at successive heights, resting against notchlike vantages in the rock that rose at each side. Once they were in, any push or shove from the far side would not budge them.

Still, they were down. Closer inspection pointed to the obvious answer.

"They've been knocked down by cattle crowding against them from *this* side," he pointed out. "That way, there was nothing to hold them. These are cattle tracks. Several must have come back to the valley, and they weren't in a mood to be stopped."

Swant looked hopeful as he understood.

"Then you think the horses will still be down there?"

"It seems reasonable. Let's go on and find out."

Another mile of gradual descent brought them to the valley, widening, stretching for a considerable distance, its outlines lost in the night. But ahead was sufficient light to make out cattle, bedded for the night, and, well to one side, the horses, moving, perhaps grazing.

There was a fresh problem as they approached. The ponies threw up their heads, watching, snorting, then began a wary retreat. Perversely they refused to respond to calls, or to permit a closer approach. That was not surprising. Horses, wild or well broken, given a taste of freedom, were apt to resist being caught and returned to the serfdom from which they had escaped.

Generally, after a few wild runs, they tired of the game and submitted, with a docile appearance that suggested that even men must appreciate that it had been all in fun. A rider on a good roundup pony was a swift inducement to reason.

Here the men were afoot, lacking bridles as well as saddles, and Blanchard had long memories of other horses that, under similar circumstances, had refused to be caught. Here there was no time for games.

"If we spread out, maybe we can herd them toward the hill," Swant suggested. "There's kind of an inside corner there, and if we can get up to them—"

"We've nothing to lose by trying," Blanchard

agreed, and they put the plan in operation. The horses continued an uneasy retreat, but their unfamiliarity with this new range enabled the men to herd them as Swant had suggested.

The test would come as they crowded in on them. If the ponies responded to long training and waited, they could be managed. If they broke, stampeding suddenly, men on foot not only could not stop them, but they might be knocked flat, even trampled in the rush.

At the last moment that happened. Blanchard heard Swant's cry, saw him sent spinning as a horse plowed at him and past. Blanchard had time for only that; then all his attention was on the animals that were dodging, snaking past him. A jump carried him on a collision course, then he was clutching wildly for a flowing mane, scrambling to get and hold a seat, in immediate danger of being brushed or bucked off. The pony's wild squeal was added testimony that this was at best a half-wild cayuse.

24

For the moment it was wholly wild, squealing with rage at any attempted curtailment of its new-won freedom. Never better than a half-tamed outlaw, the pony would be difficult to control even with saddle and bridle. Such animals were common; reasonably docile when regularly ridden, they had to be mastered all over again after even a short period of idleness.

Blanchard was no stranger to such cayuses, but ordinarily he was firmly seated in a saddle, reins in hand, and which he missed most was hard to judge. He managed to cling and hold a moment, shoving forward, both hands in the heavy mane, knees pinching for what purchase such scissoring provided.

Predictably, the pony allowed him no respite. Still shrilling its fury, it went into an established routine—plunging, bucking, whirling—conduct almost always effective in dislodging a rider. With no bridle for control, Blanchard was doubly handicapped, the outlaw free to cavort as it pleased.

But the man was as desperate as the horse, and as Indians had proved, there were some advantages in riding bareback, stretched along an animal's neck, conforming to its every twist and turn, making yourself a part of the total. Blanchard held fast.

Whether he could cling long enough to outlast the pony's rage was the immediate question. Such a horse, repeatedly tamed, usually bucked hard for a few moments, testing a new rider, venting its feelings. If those jumps achieved no result, it generally subsided with the resigned air of having done its duty.

This occasion was different—there was no firm hand exerting an iron pressure on the bit in its mouth, no raking spurs to punish and warn. The horse was fresh, and there were any number of ways to harass or dislodge a rider. It seemed to be in a mood to try them all.

Running furiously, it reversed itself with a twisting jump, heading back the way it had come with no slackening of speed. A fresh squeal of fury blasted on the night as it found itself still burdened, and Blanchard, lifted, all but tossed aside, wondered if he could hold for another such jump and twist. Then, sensing a new purposefulness in the pony's rush, terror broke in a clammy sweat across his face.

An average cayuse might show ornery on such occasions, always trying for a victory it did not really expect, resignedly accepting its role. But there were exceptions—occasional brutes in the full sense of the term, possessed of a killer instinct, going berserk when the opportunity offered. He was riding such an animal.

Swant had tried to stop the rush of the horse herd, taking as desperate a chance as Blanchard and going down before the wild plunge of an animal. Clearly dazed and hurt, instinct had brought him back on his feet, staggering blindly. A disastrous effort, directing attention where otherwise he would have gone unnoticed. A triumphant squeal from Blanchard's cayuse emphasized its intention.

Whether Swant heard or noticed was impossible to tell. He took another unsteady step, then faltered and sprawled. The lift and plunge of bone and muscle between Blanchard's clutching knees seemed to increase.

Years before, Blanchard had come upon a tableau of the wild, close enough to witness though too far away to intervene. A rattlesnake coiled and rendered savage in the blind fury of late summer, the shedding of its skin, and its sense of helplessness while the new one remained fresh and tender, had threatened a young colt. At such times a diamondback became doubly menacing, striking unreasoningly.

A stallion had raced to the rescue. Disdaining the threat of that flattened head and the coil ready to be unleashed, it had come down upon the reptile with all hoofs bunched, squealing its defiance, stomping repeatedly until scarcely a remnant remained.

This killer was berserk, and Swant would be its target. Blanchard knew, even if he survived its gyrations, clinging to its back, his weight would not impede or even slow the horse's dance of death.

Space remained between man and cayuse, though it was being licked away as by fire in grass. Time, little enough, was fast running out.

Blanchard's mind seemed attuned, working with equal speed. It was a long chance, a course of desperation, but there was no other choice, no second way. For the moment, intent on its new objective, the horse was running, wasting no time or effort in trying to rid itself of him.

He had a rawhide string in a pocket—a thong a yard long, which he had helped himself to back at the cavern, from among the supplies. Whether there was time, or if he could work it in any case, he was far from certain. But, aside from the added risk of giving up his hold and being spilled, to be swung upon and hammered in turn, there was nothing to lose by trying.

His left hand was wrapped in the mane. Letting go with his right, he pulled out the thong and held it by both ends, shaking out the slack into as wide a loop as possible. Then he stretched along the pony's neck, leaning far forward, balancing precariously. He made a final lunge even as the horse was trying to do the same, an outreaching shove. There could be no second chance, no time, nor would the outlaw allow another.

Ordinarily it would have been beyond his ability, but man and horse were both above themselves. Blanchard felt the noose pull tight as it closed around nose and jaws, and he leaned back hard, clinging to the ends, twisting, exerting all the strength he could bring to bear.

Swant, dazed, was directly ahead, trying uncertainly to raise his head.

Again the cayuse squealed, rage choked to a terror of pain as the thong closed cruelly on its tender nose. At such a spot a horse was peculiarly vulnerable. It swerved, staggered, and came back almost on its heels. Swant, forgotten, suddenly cognizant of his peril, crawled frantically and regained his feet.

Blanchard sat upright for the first time since the beginning of his ride, easing the pressure of the thong, speaking soothingly. Trembling, eyes rolling, as chastened as it was cowed by those moments of helpless agony, the cayuse stood.

25

The night was wearing out as they neared the cavern. There had been time, as Blanchard had hoped, but none to spare. The twisting descent into the valley had been a slow one, but climbing up and out was worse, though by then he and Swant were in control of the horses, herding them, riding comfortably.

A horse is an intelligent animal, often clever, many times friendly, trusting and trustworthy; as with men, much depends on the individual. But there is such a thing as horse sense, and, once learned, a horse remembers a lesson.

The mottled gray cayuse that Blanchard had drawn was taking its chastisement to heart. Not only had this rider stayed with the gray despite its best efforts to be rid of him, but it had punished the horse savagely while bringing it under control.

It moved obediently, completely docile, requiring little more than a word, the touch of guiding knees, though a loose loop of the rawhide around its nose and jaws was there to implement a command at need.

The other horses had not run far. Blanchard rounded them up, aided by his mount, skilled at such a chore and now anxious to please.

Swant would hobble about for a while on a sprained ankle. Aside from a bruised cheek and a sense of wooziness that was wearing off by the time Blanchard returned with the ponies, he was not much hurt. Supplied with a matching type of bridle and a gentler horse, he was able to ride.

He was at once grateful but contrite, foreseeing at least in part how his mishap had worsened an already tenuous situation.

"I can still put up a fight," he assured Blanchard earnestly. "But I can't hide this bad foot or this ornament on my phiz. From the way it feels, it ain't no beauty mark. Everybody'll notice—and want answers. I reckon it'll upset whatever scheme you had in mind."

"We'll just have to go at it from a different angle," Blanchard admitted. His plan was ruined, a basically sound scheme no longer usable.

Explanations could neither be postponed nor avoided. Swant might hide out, but that in itself would arouse suspicion and precipitate a crisis. Blanchard could see nothing for it but to alter his plan to fit the circumstance, and bluff or fight as the occasion demanded.

They left the tired horses where they had been originally held, since the location was reasonably close and served the purpose. Swant, insisting that he could walk, managed a few hobbling steps; then, sweating, he accepted Blanchard's arm and shoulder to stumble the rest of the way to the cave.

A grayness to the east heralded the coming dawn. Blanchard studied the sky with resignation. From all the signs, there would be a short period of sun, shut away by a spreading haze. Before another dawn there would be more snow, and that storm was likely to be a big one. Time was running out.

Had any choice remained, it was lost as they discovered that the others were stirring, awake earlier than usual. That was easy to understand—the excitement of a promised bonanza inflamed their minds.

Though just awake, Blanchard and Swant's absence had been discovered. Lundy glowered from the cave mouth as they approached.

"And what have you two been up to?" he demanded, but his regard for Swant was the darker. With Gregor lost, he was suddenly in danger of being badly outnumbered.

"We've been rounding up the horses," Blanchard answered. "They're back where they were. It wasn't easy," he amplified, with a glance at Swant and his limp.

The reply was so unexpected that it was disconcerting. Since the answer could readily be verified, and seemed an invaluable service, Lundy was at a loss.

"The rest of us are supposed to know what's going on," he growled.

"I thought of telling you what we had in mind, but it seemed wiser not to spoil your beauty sleep." Blanchard shrugged.

A new tenseness gripped everyone. They asked no further questions, but that Lundy's remaining companion had worked in concert with Blanchard was significant. Its meaning was not fully clear but the implications were not lost on Lundy. Eve eyed Swant anxiously, concern in her face. He clearly had told the truth about her feelings.

"What about that gold you was to show us?" Lundy demanded.

"It will be right there and waiting," Blanchard returned. "I'm hungry and sleepy. Let's have some breakfast, then I want a nap. I reckon Swant needs one, too. It'll need to be full daylight, back behind these hills, before we can see to find things."

Eager but as wary as a wolf scenting a trap, Lundy made no protest at the delay, nor did Kearns. He too was anxious, but the atmosphere had changed. Kearns would stand with Lundy, with the unhappy realization that he had worked himself into a corner and had no choice. But Blanchard was in command. However they resented that and however sure they were to fight to regain supremacy, Blanchard's control was for the moment, accepted by everyone.

Jeb Cooley was showing a steady improvement. Time was a healer, and good food, coupled with the stimulus of Mavis and Blanchard to side him, was having an excellent effect. His eyes, watching the others, held a glint of amusement as he ate. Blanchard was as much of a surprise to him as to them, but only in his unorthodox method. Cooley had known what to expect overall.

But he looked startled when Blanchard tossed a bone at the fire and questioned him casually.

"You've got some dynamite, Jeb?"

Cooley was too old a campaigner to betray that such a subject had been discussed before.

"Dynamite? Guess I've a stick or so left somewhere around."

"I'll need it," Blanchard said. "As soon as I've had a nap."

Cooley eyed him admiringly. The others were increasingly uneasy, thrown off stride by such openness. They had an unhappy conviction that they were witnessing a sort of magic act, with everything exposed, but that he would somehow pull a rabbit from an empty hat.

Blanchard slept an hour, then wakened as he had set himself to do, considerably refreshed. The stimulus of such a contest made his blood course faster.

The anxiety in the eyes of Mavis and Jeb, of Eve and Eva, and of Swant had a sobering effect. The lines by now were clearly drawn, though nothing had been said between Lundy and Swant, no challenge given. With grim understanding, his defection, at least in spirit, was accepted.

"We'll need ropes," Blanchard said. "There's some rough going ahead. And lanterns."

Silverman grunted his surprise.

"Lanterns? You mean the stuff's somewhere back in here—in this cave?"

"That would make things handy, if it was that easy. But to reach it we have to go through the cave."

Suspicion and distrust flared in Lundy's eyes.

"But there ain't no way through," he protested. "If you're trying to fool us . . ."

Beyond much doubt they had tried to explore, but lacking lanterns, the search had not been rewarding. It would have been easy to miss the side cave, and only chance or luck had enabled Blanchard to glimpse that high up, revealing gleam of light.

"I've promised to lead you to the stuff and show you," he pointed out. "If you don't want to go, then we might as well take the horses and head out."

"Oh, hell." Lundy was frustrated with his sense of helplessness, his rage near the explosive point. "Get on with it."

There was further argument as to who should go or remain behind. It was agreed that the women and Eva should stay with Cooley, but Swant insisted on coming, despite his ankle. Lundy was clearly of two minds about him. There was no one else to side him, but he was suddenly doubtful of Swant's loyalty.

Taking advantage of the confusion, Cooley contrived to slip a couple of long, thin packets to Blanchard.

"All set and ready to create a diversion," he whispered. "Cap and fuse fixed. Just light the fuse." He had no chance to say more.

Blanchard pocketed the dynamite gratefully. Cooley had understood something of what he had in mind and prepared the sticks for instant use.

Blanchard knew just enough of high explosives to regard them with a healthy respect.

Blanchard led the way, with Cooley close at his heels and Swant behind him. Kearns followed with another lantern, Cloud and Silverman lost in the darkness to the rear. Grotesque shadows assumed even more fantastic forms as they made a ghostly accompaniment. Blanchard bypassed the side cave, with none of the others the wiser.

Climbing, Swant stumbled and clutched at Lundy, to be cursed for his clumsiness. Blanchard resisted the impulse to grapple Lundy for his gun in the confusion. His move would stand its best chance when they had sighted the strike and were avid to get their hands on it.

It was doubtful if Cooley had come this far into the recesses or made the same discovery. Jeb had had other objectives on his mind, and then other enemies with which to contend. There were a lot of ironic twists to so strange a summer.

"Watch your step," Blanchard cautioned. Then he pointed to the far gleam of daylight. "There's the back door."

They followed eagerly, no longer doubting. Lundy growled an order, insisting on going first. His face showed curiously pale when Blanchard squeezed through the rocky fissure and was alongside. The looming face of the glacier, almost within reach, was startling enough, just as its overhang seemed to threaten imminent disaster. But the pit at their feet, half a hundred feet straight down, had surprised and shaken Lundy. Clearly he had no head or stomach for heights.

Swant looked about stolidly, panting. Kearns stared, amazed. Then, despite the dusting of snow that still shrouded the face of the glacier, he was first to understand. "Ice!"

"Glacier," Blanchard confirmed. "Miles of it, most likely, stretching back up a valley, filling it. More than likely it overtopped the cave a few centuries ago. Lately, as you can see, it's been melting, getting smaller, even retreating instead of grinding ahead."

It was clear enough that none of the others had ever glimpsed the ice mass, hidden in its valley behind the hills. Kearns swore with mounting excitement and understanding, but Lundy, who at best had been only an amateur prospector, was slower to understand.

"What the hell good is ice?" he demanded. "I thought you said there was gold—"

Volubly eager, Kearns pointed below.

"Can't you see, man? It's right down there! It has to be. That's a pocket, a deadend where all the rock and debris and gold that the glacier has scraped loose and shoved along, all the way down from the high mountains, has been trapped. And now that the ice has finally melted back a bit, it's uncovered, within reach. . . ."

The rest of them were suddenly frantic with understanding, anxious to get down and prove it for themselves. The necessity of the ropes was apparent. There was no other way down or up. Two lengths of rope, each the size of a lariat, reached nicely when knotted together.

Kearns was lowered first, this time with Lundy offering no protest. Not waiting for permission or assistance, Silverman and Cloud descended the rope next, hand over hand, half sliding, careless even of a rope burn in their eagerness. Blanchard, Swant, and Lundy, standing and peering down into the pit, still awaited their chance on the rope. Caution was forgotten as Kearns kicked hard, loosening some object that showed rough underfoot. He bent down, then came up, clutching it, his wild yowl of exultation turned back and smothered by the surrounding walls.

"Gold!" Kearns chortled. "The real quill! Heavy as the heart of a man facing the noose! As pure as that of the maiden he deceived!" He was waxing almost poetic. "Talk about a bonanza!"

Lundy's eyes were glittering, but though plainly pleased with such confirmation, he was as controlled and deadly as a puma crouching on a limb, waiting the moment when its spring would be most deadly. That quality had given him leadership, and unlike Kearns or most of the others, he was deadly efficient, not inclined to babble at a moment requiring action.

He swung abruptly at Blanchard, bringing up his gun. With no word of warning he squeezed the trigger, the range point blank.

26

Blanchard had a lightning-swift flash of understanding, time to comprehend but not to resist. The gold was there, as the others had confirmed. Blanchard had led them to it, and thus had outlived his usefulness. Lundy was vengeful, though even that was secondary. What counted was to regain control, with no waste of time.

The gun clicked uselessly. Lundy's glance, cold as the matching glacier along its barrel, shifted in sudden shock from Blanchard's face to the weapon. He triggered frantically, the double-action rasping loud against the sudden silence. Loud, but with a continuing emptiness.

Swant's voice recalled him to reality. The hate and frustration of years lent a matching quality of deadliness. He in turn was eyeing Lundy along the leveled barrel of a gun.

"An empty gun can't shoot, Tom! That's what you told me, remember? So I traded with you—back there in the dark. *This* one's loaded!"

Lundy glared with frantic understanding. His glacial calm was gone. He struck frantically with the gun in his hand, reaching in an overlong stroke, missing as Swant jerked aside. Overextended, forgetful for an instant of the narrow shelf on which he was poised, Lundy slipped. The next instant another yowl, strangely akin to the one emitted by Kearns yet as alien as death from life, shattered the silence as he plunged into the pit.

Then silence returned, with even the scream lost like a whisper amid the vastness. Silverman, scrambling wildly, had barely made it out of the way as Lundy hurtled down. The trio at the bottom stared in disbelief at Lundy's broken body. The nugget in Kearns's hand thudded audibly as it slipped from nerveless fingers.

Blanchard drew a slow breath. Relief was like reprieve. He had been prepared for trouble, but the swift ruthlessness of Lundy's attack had been impossible to guard against.

"I—I'd like to say thanks—" His tongue was thick, slurring the words. Swant's face, hard as the surrounding stone, slowly relaxed.

"Sort of evens us up for what you did with that horse set to stomp me," he returned. "Here." He thrust the revolver into Blanchard's hand. "They've still got guns." He nodded toward the frozen trio below.

Blanchard accepted the gun mechanically. For the moment it was superfluous. Kearns and his henchmen were gamblers, but they were not killers, nor possessed of the relentless qualities that had driven

Lundy. They were suddenly frightened and abject, even the golden hoard at their feet no longer able to move them. The knowledge that they would never possess it lent a hollow quality to Kearns's voice.

"If you'll give us a hand up—we'll send the guns first, or whatever you say. I sure didn't bargain for anything like this."

"You wanted it, so you might as well enjoy it while you have the chance." Blanchard was coldly dispassionate. He had been prepared to make a move, to catch the opposition by surprise and blast loose that massive outthrust of ice, dropping it to fill and cover the cleared space below to a depth of probably a score of feet; sufficient at least to require several more years for melting, a cover to protect the gold from any and everyone.

He had faced the possbility that it might be necessary to use such a desperate blast, its outfall perhaps catching the others. It was a relief that nothing so drastic had been required, but when the balance lay between Mavis and her father, Eve and Eva, to say nothing of Swant and himself, he had been prepared to use what might be the only possible weapon.

With manpower to spare, they had held onto the rope as the others went down it. He tied the end now to a thumb of stone conveniently at hand. Ascending the rope under their own power was likely to prove a chore for the trio, Kearns in particular, but Blanchard had a notion that, lacking any choice, they would manage. But however driven by lust for gold, they would be unable to burden themselves on the climb with pocketsful of nuggets.

For the first time he was able to get a good view of the crest of hill above. Beyond the fissure from which they had crawled it rose steeply again, almost sheer, but with a rope to aid, the others should be able to reach the top, to circle and make a descent back to the valley. It would be a time-consuming chore, allowing more than enough time for the rest of them to saddle and ride out. He explained to Kearns.

"You can keep your guns. You may need them to get meat. If you keep moving, you should beat the heavy snows and get back out—to somewhere new. That way, you won't be on our trail or pester again. It's better than you deserve."

The others did not plead. They were staring, ashen-faced, as Blanchard and Swant lowered themselves through the crevice. Swant pointed out the obvious weakness of the plan, which Kearns had clearly been quick to perceive.

"They'll have to go in the dark, but they won't be far behind. They'll sure do their best to catch up. And with guns . . ."

"Take your lantern and keep moving," Blanchard instructed. "I'll use one stick of dynamite as I'd planned from the start. It shouldn't take much to jar enough overhead to close the way in or out." He was already thrusting a charge into a crack in the rock, striking a match. "If this works, they won't follow directly."

"You sure think of everything," Swant commended, and went hastily ahead, seemingly not impaired by his injured ankle. The fuse alight, Blanchard followed.

They had reached a safe distance when the concussion of the blast made the lanterns flicker. Then, as the sliding and grinding subsided, the last of the daylight was shut away.

Swant was still ahead when Blanchard delayed to explore more fully the side cave, guarded still by the dead man. He had no doubt that the skeleton was Slade Tatum. An imaginative, even brilliant man, considering all that he had accomplished. But he had come with final success almost within grasp, to the end of a crooked trail deep in the heart of a mountain, his last accomplice turning traitor in the hope of total possession.

27

Reunion was almost as though they had parted days or weeks before, instead of hardly more than an hour. Jeb Cooley, on his feet and pacing, however slowly and in a restricted space, swung about with sudden eagerness. The women stared, then, certain of the absence of their enemies, Mavis cried out and ran to Blanchard. Eve, a sob in her throat, welcomed Swant almost as warmly.

Cooley watched approvingly, an eyebrow lifted in question and resignation.

"Guess there's not much need for me to add a welcomin' word," he observed. "Only I'm like a gopher penned too long in the same hole. Got sort of an itch."

"Kearns and his friends are taking the long way around," Blanchard explained. "Likely they're as tired of our company as we were of theirs. We'll get the horses and start back, as soon as we've eaten." Almost in afterthought, he tossed a pouch to Cooley. "You'll want this now, of course."

Cooley picked it up mechanically, but he was in no hurry to open the drawstring. Mavis wondered if it contained coins, since nuggets would not make such a sound. Judging from the fancy beadwork that covered the pouch, it was Indian in design and construction, soft white rawhide discolored by age.

"You're not implyin' that Lundy is travelin' with Kearns?" Jeb protested. "Buzzards and crows ain't that much birds of a feather."

Swant took it upon himself to answer, his eyes narrowly on Eve.

"He's dead. Showed his hand the minute he thought he had the gold, turning his gun on Blanchard and pullin' trigger."

Blanchard supplied what he left out.

"Joe had managed to trade guns with him along the way. And since Lundy had made him go with an empty gun..."

The words seemed to hang in air while the others digested the implications. Swant added a final word.

"Resulted in a mixup there on the edge of that hole. Lundy slipped."

Eve's eyes, tensely on his own during the recital, fell away, a sigh escaping her. She shook her head as though closing an episode, manifestly with relief rather than tears. Only Eva, with a child's directness, voiced the common thought.

"I'm glad! Now you're free of him, Mommy—all of us are." Her glance took in Swant, coloring uncertainly as he met her look.

Jeb Cooley interposed with a tactful question.

"You're way ahead of me, Harry, and the girls,

too. Your story fair trips on the tongue, only we don't know what you're talking about."

"But you explored this cave enough to find the side room—the one that's occupied?" Blanchard asked.

"That much I did." He shifted the pouch from one hand to the other. "You're telling me there was something beyond?"

"A back door to the cave, you might call it. That was what gave me the idea—that and the nugget your tame pack rat presented me with, which I used to whet their excitement."

"I'd wondered where you got hold of that nugget," Cooley conceded. "You sure put it to good use."

Blanchard sketched what had happened—the glacier that filled its valley, now in a slow retreat, the precipice above the pit, and the eagerness of the men to descend into the hole, to get at long last their hands on the gold. The others listened with interest, a glint of amusement unhidden in Jeb's eyes.

"And they figured they'd really found my strike? And mighty rich, at that?"

"I figured the same," Blanchard reminded. "Only as to your strike, I knew better."

"Fooled you that much—and them, too." Cooley grinned wearily. "I *did* find that back door and have a look at that ice and the nice hole it left by meltin' back. But as for gold—you've heard of saltin' a mine, Harry. The rest of you too, of course."

"What're you getting at, Jeb?" It was Blanchard's turn to be puzzled. Manifestly there was something here that he had overlooked.

"Everybody figured I was prospectin' for gold," Cooley pointed out. "Didn't hurt for them to think that if they liked, and nobody would have believed me if I'd contradicted them. Only I wasn't. I was more or less trailin' Slade Tatum's herd of cattle, since Slade went along with them."

Blanchard's interest quickened, though he had already pieced those clues together.

"I'd done a lot of wondering about Tatum, picked up a few pointers now and then, and sort of put them together. Startin' with two things that tallied: One, that Tatum had been down California way before he reached this north country; and second, that there'd been a big robbery of a special messenger in San Francisco—a tidy fortune in diamonds. Matched stones, all of them several carats in size, just off a ship from somewhere in Europe, bound for a new owner somewhere back East.

"That robbery had taken place not too long before Slade Tatum showed up in town and then on my ranch. And the stolen jewels never have been found, despite a lot of searching and a mighty big reward offered. I speculated that maybe Slade Tatum had engineered that robbery, which took some doing. Only trouble with such a haul, of course, is that havin' such a fortune can be a problem. For one thing, the law's on your trail. And maybe worse, others as lackin' in scruple as yourself would follow such a scent, same as a fox at a hen yard."

He grinned at the tenseness with which the others hung on his words.

"I surmised that Tatum was the robber, and that

he'd got as far as my ranch, but by that time a rival gang of thieves were closin' in on him, determined to steal what he'd stolen and maybe even more lackin' in scruples, should murder be required. He was in a fix. To go any farther posed a threat of being overtaken and robbed, most likely killed.

"So he came up with a right ingenious scheme for transportin' his haul to a new and remote place, using a method nobody'd be likely to suspect. If he could just reach the border, he figured to be all right.

"So he bought that herd of cattle, slapped his brand on them, makin' use of the squeeze pen on my land for the job. The brandin' made a good cover for the real job. Holding a critter so it couldn't move, two or three of them could make a quick cut into the fleshy part of the dewlap, shove a stone out of sight, close the incision with a length of fine wire twisted through the skin, and repeat the process with the next animal. All marks would be concealed by the long hair. And the evidence shows that it worked."

Jeb's recital tallied with what Blanchard had deduced. Cooley went on. "Tatum came mighty close to succeeding. Everybody thought he was crazy, and when he drove off a herd of cattle, into wild country, it sure looked like he was crazy. I guess it took those others quite a while to figure out. By that time he'd reached this country, built another squeeze pen, and run most of the stock through it, retrievin' the diamonds.

"But either they caught up with him, or else one of his own crew turned traitor. Once I found traces of the herd still back in this country, I knew I was on the right track. I reckon you figured out the rest, Harry, quite some time ago."

"It took you to really come up with the answer, to give me the right clues." Blanchard nodded. "I did find a stone on a steer we butchered. Tatum mustn't have had time to finish."

Cooley juggled the pouch reflectively.

"I left this right where Tatum had it, back in that little side room," he added. "With others doggin' my steps, matters got sort of touchy for a spell. But I managed to get those homin' pigeons away, and I knew you'd come, same as you'd promised. All I had to do was hold out."

Mavis had listened intently. She kissed her father impulsively, swung to Blanchard, but then, coloring, drew back a step.

"I'm proud of you—both of my men," she asserted sweepingly.

"I don't know much about diamonds, but I suspect this amounts to quite a fortune," Cooley observed. "I wouldn't doubt that the reward for finding them is still in effect, so it'll add up to a good summer's work."

"And you made a gold strike in the bargain, even if you weren't prospecting," Eve pointed out.

Cooley's smile was whimsical.

"There'll be something of the reward for everybody, so we'll do all right," he promised. "But don't get your hopes too high. I knew all along this wasn't gold country. If Kearns had been half as smart as he figured, he'd have known it, too."

"But there is gold, back under that ice," Swant protested.

"Sure. Didn't you hear what I said about saltin' a claim? I figured I might be bothered by others, and there's nothing like a bit of dust in the eyes—especially gold dust. So I brought along a handful of nuggets. One got lost, but that rat found it and gave it to you, Harry, so that part worked out fine.

"I used the rest to throw down from the top of that ledge, to salt that hole. Didn't work out to be necessary, but you never can tell."

Swant was still incredulous.

"But Kearns had a nugget as big as his fist—"

"Kearns," Jeb pointed out patiently, "was so excited he couldn't see straight, much less think the same way. Any chunk of rock was gold to him. You'd salted the notion in their minds, Harry, as sure as I'd salted the claim. Speakin' of salt, I'm hungry. Let's eat, then get going. I wouldn't want those pigeons to have flown in vain."